GUARDING GRACE

THE GOLD COAST RETRIEVERS

ANN OMASTA

Dedicated to my wonderful parents.
Thank you for loving me almost as much as you love your Golden
Retrievers.

FREE DOWNLOAD!

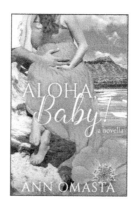

Escape to the enchanting Hawaiian Islands in Leilani's heart-warming tale of friendship, love, and triumph after heartbreak.

Join Ann Omasta's VIP reader group and tell us where to send your free novella. You can unsubscribe at any time.

Visit annomasta.com to claim your free copy!

race Wilson knew it would probably be smart to deny the request of the precious freckle-faced little girl gazing adoringly up at her, but a big part of her wanted to grant the child's wish. Her sweet daughter, Clover, rarely asked for anything, so when she did, Grace usually did her best to make it happen.

Clover sensed her mother's hesitation and went even deeper into adorable cherub mode. "Pleeeease, Mommy. I've always wanted a Golden Wetweevah puppy."

Grace smiled down at her pint-sized mini-me. Clover's teacher would not approve of Grace's failure to correct Clover's "R" pronunciation, but it was so ridiculously cute, she opted to let it slide. Grace savored having her little girl be little. Besides, Clover only slipped back into that particular habit when she was super excited about something.

Clover turned up the charm even further and gave her mother the full-court press. Her huge cornflower blue eyes pleaded up at Grace. When she smiled, the gap from her missing front tooth reminded Grace just how fast the child was changing.

"I promise to take super-great care of her. I'll feed her, and walk her, and brush her..." Clover paused, obviously deep in thought, trying to figure out what else a puppy needed. Excitement lit up her eyes right before she added, "I'll play ball with her."

"A puppy is a huge responsibility." Grace tried to insert a significant degree of seriousness into her tone, even though the little girl had already almost convinced her.

Clover pondered Grace's words for a moment before deciding. "I know, and I think I'm ready. I'll be a great Mommy to the puppy because I learned how to Mommy from the best one in the whole wide world!"

Tears of happiness pooled in Grace's lower lids. She hadn't been at all sure about moving halfway across the country to the Northern California coastline and raising a child on her own. When she had found out she was pregnant, her long-term boyfriend had gotten scared and dumped her. She had then turned to her religious parents, who shunned her for getting pregnant out of wedlock.

Deciding she and the baby would have to figure out how to make it on their own, she had packed her belongings, collected her meager savings, and moved to the most beautiful place she could imagine: Redwood Cove, California, along the beautiful Gold Coast. The picturesque resort town was nestled by the ocean about an hour north of San Francisco. It seemed like the perfect place to raise a child––even if she had to do it all by herself.

Deep down, she knew she had made the right decision in moving here. She was also confident that she was doing a fantastic job of raising Clover, but hearing affirmation from the child herself was immensely gratifying. "Thanks, sweetheart." She gave her daughter a watery-eyed grin.

Seeing her mother's tears, Clover's expression turned forlorn. "Did I do something wrong?"

"No, sweet girl, you make everything better," Grace told her earnestly. Clover beamed at the praise, and Grace made a snap decision. "Let's call Marlene to see if she'll let us have a puppy."

Clover's eyes lit up with excitement because she knew as well as Grace did that their landlord, Marlene, would grant their request. They had been lucky enough to rent the empty apartment on the side of Marlene's clapboard row house ever since Grace had arrived pregnant, scared, and alone in Redwood Cove.

Marlene had immediately taken lonely and frightened Grace under her wing. Marlene had three children of her own, whom she handled like a pro. She quickly became Grace's adopted aunt, best friend, confidant, and––once Clover was born––babysitter. Grace couldn't imagine how she would have survived the last few years if she hadn't been lucky enough to meet Marlene in those first days after her arrival in California.

Finding an empty bench that looked out over the crystal-clear water, the mother and daughter duo sat down to call Marlene. When Grace located her phone and pulled it from her purse, Clover said, "Put it on speakerphone, please, because I want to talk to her, too."

Grace complied with her request, knowing that meant there was absolutely no way Marlene would deny them the puppy. Their landlord had turned into their family-by-choice, and she had an even bigger soft spot for Clover than Grace did.

"Good morning, Sunshines," Marlene greeted them when she answered her phone.

"Morning, Aunt Mar," Clover greeted the other woman in her life. Unable to contain herself long enough for any more pleasantries, Clover asked, "Is it okay if we get a puppy?'

Obviously surprised by the out-of-the-blue request and

stalling for time, Marlene answered, "Oh, my... a puppy." She paused for a moment before asking, "Is your mom on board with this, Sweetie?"

Feeling grateful that Marlene was looking out for her, Grace answered, "Only if it's not a problem for you." She wanted to give the woman an out if she didn't want them to have a pet. They had never had an official lease in writing, and the prospect of getting a puppy had never before been discussed.

Grace didn't like putting the woman on the spot like this, so she offered, "Maybe we should discuss it later."

"Is this what y-o-u w-a-n-t?" Grace smiled at Marlene's spelled words. They had long used the tactic of spelling out words they didn't want Clover to understand––especially around the child's birthday.

"Yes, she wants it!" Clover beamed. She was obviously proud of herself for learning their previously-baffling secret language.

Both women chuckled at her glee. "Well, I guess we can kiss that secret code language goodbye." Grace smiled down at her adorable little girl.

"When did you learn to spell so well?" Marlene asked the child, pride bubbling in her voice.

"I've been learning for a while now," Clover told her seriously. "I was saving it to surprise you."

"Well, that you did, little one." Grace could practically hear Marlene smiling through the phone. Turning serious, she asked, "You're sure, Grace?"

"Not completely," Grace answered honestly, before adding, "But I think it's time we added to our little family."

"Okay, then, I can't wait to meet your new puppy," Marlene told them.

That confirmation was all the little girl needed. She

jumped up from their bench and let out a loud "Whoop!" of excitement, which echoed out across the shimmery water.

When their laughter died down, Marlene said, "Wow! I think I might have been able to hear your gleeful shout without our phone connection."

"We gotta go, Aunt Mar. We're going to get our puppy!" Clover yelled. "Bye!" She grabbed the phone from her surprised mother to end the call. "Let's go pick out our puppy!" she half-shouted.

A momentary shadow of doubt swept over Grace about this decision now that it seemed to be quickly becoming a reality, but the giddy expression on her child's face told her that she was in too deep to turn back now.

After a quick Google search and a phone call, Grace had an appointment scheduled with Carol Graves, the friendly woman who loved to show off pictures of her adorable golden puppies when she came into the grocery bakery where Grace worked.

"Let's go meet the newest addition to our family," Grace suggested, before standing and taking Clover's hand within her own. The happy duo set off on what would soon turn out to be one of the greatest adventures of their lives.

*G*race knew her daughter would be immediately smitten with the puppies, but she hadn't expected her own strong reaction to the adorable, roly-poly poof balls. As soon as they entered the enclosure where the puppies were playing and napping, the tiny animals pounced.

It was cuteness-overload as the two humans squatted down and were attacked by the golden-haired, real-life teddy bears. The puppies were drawn to Clover. The little girl giggled with pure happiness as they snuffled, licked, cuddled, and nipped at her.

"Can we have them all?" She turned her bright, hope-filled blue eyes up at her mother.

"No. Just one." Grace used her best, firm mom-voice. "They won't always be this little, you know. They are going to grow into big dogs." She had been half-expecting Clover to whine about her response, but the little girl seemed to understand that they truly only had room for one puppy.

"How am I ever going to pick which one?" Clover looked up at her mother, obviously seeking her guidance and wisdom.

Grace wasn't sure how to answer because she had just been wondering the same thing. All of the puppies were soft, sweet, and utterly adorable. How were they supposed to decide which one to take home with them?

"How about if you sit down and get to know the puppies, while I talk about the adoption details with Mrs. Graves?" Grace used her hand to indicate the woman before leaning down near her daughter's ear to add, "Maybe one of the puppies will pick you."

At the hope-filled gaze Clover beamed up at her, Grace silently prayed that would be the case. She had read once that it was better to let the puppy pick the family, but she had never been through the process of selecting one before, so she wasn't positive if it actually worked that way.

Grace had already been impressed by the living conditions of the plump, obviously-healthy, and well-cared-for puppies, but when she began talking to the breeder, she became even more confident in her decision. Carol asked all the right questions to ensure Grace and Clover would provide the puppy with a good home, making it obvious she truly cared about the puppies and their long-term wellbeing.

When the mama dog, Rita, came over and gently shoved her head into Grace's hand, Grace kneeled down to talk to her. "Aren't you a beauty?" she commented, rubbing the dogs ears, which made the dog's tail wag slowly. "You did a great job with your sweet babies, and I promise to be the best Mommy I can, if you let me adopt one of your pups."

Carol closely watched Grace's interaction with Rita before saying, "We normally only sell our pups to people planning to train them as service, rescue, or therapy dogs, but I have a good feeling about you two." Carol gave Grace a kind smile, nodding her head in silent approval for them to get a puppy.

Although Grace was nervous about the long-term financial commitment, since she knew dog food, veterinarian bills, and other miscellaneous expenses would add up to a substantial amount, Grace decided she would scrimp even more on her own expenses to find the money to properly care for the dog. When she turned to watch Clover giggle as the puppies attacked her, there was almost no doubt left in her mind. She felt confident this was the right decision for their little family.

After the details were finalized, Carol smiled down at Clover and said, "You're going to make a wonderful big sister to the lucky puppy that gets to go home with you."

"You think so?" Clover couldn't hide the excitement in her voice over the woman's assessment and the idea of becoming a big sister. She obviously hadn't thought about it that way before.

"I know so," the woman assured her. "Being a big sister is a huge responsibility, but I think you're ready."

Clover nodded. "I am," she added solemnly, obviously sensing the importance of this moment.

Grace smiled at the woman for saying precisely the right things before joining her daughter on the floor. "Have you chosen one?"

Surprising her mother with her decisiveness, Clover picked up one of the squirming puppies. "This one." Turning to the woman standing behind them, she furrowed her brow before asking. "She's a girl, right?"

"That is a female," the woman confirmed, making the child visibly sag with relief.

"Good, 'cause I always wanted a little sister, not a little brother... yuck!" Clover wrinkled her tiny, freckled nose in distaste at the idea.

"What made you choose her?" the woman asked the little girl, with true curiosity about the answer shining through on her face.

Turning to look at her mom, Clover asked, "You know how Mrs. Mallory always gives me a star sticker on my papers when I do a great job?"

"Yes," Grace answered, intrigued with where her daughter was going with this.

"Well, look-y here..." The little girl pointed the front half of the plump golden puppy towards her mother.

Grace looked at the white patch of fur on the puppy's chest and nodded, still perplexed by what her daughter was getting at.

"She has a white star right on her neck, like a permanent necklace!" Clover nearly shouted. "That must mean she's the best puppy of all."

Unable to argue with her child's logic, Grace nodded her agreement with the decision.

"Excellent choice," the breeder weighed in with her approval.

Puffing up with pride at the woman's praise, Clover plopped the puppy down in her lap. The small animal curled itself into an adorable furball on Clover's crossed legs, gave a stuttered and contented sigh, and promptly fell asleep.

With that simple gesture of trust, their fate was sealed.

3

*A*s soon as they left, Grace called to schedule an appointment for the puppy with Dr. Keller, the veterinarian who came to the grocery every Friday to get donuts for his staff.

After a quick trip to the pet supply store, which turned into a three-hour ordeal, they marveled at how much stuff such a tiny animal needed. Okay, perhaps the puppy didn't *need* it all, but both she and Clover had gotten a bit swept away in their enthusiasm. It was fun having a new family member to care for.

They bought large-breed puppy food, house-training pads, a pretty collar embroidered with colorful flowers, a bright purple leash, a red bouncy ball, a pillowy soft wool dog bed, several squeaky toys, puppy treats shaped like bones, and magenta plastic dishes for food and water.

As she struggled to carry their purchases inside the apartment, while Clover carried the puppy cradled in her arms like a baby, Grace wondered if they had gone completely overboard. Clover spread out the fuzzy blanket from the puppies' enclosure that the kind breeder had given them.

"This is so you'll have familiar smells and not feel homesick for your other Mom and siblings," Clover informed the puppy in a serious tone.

The puppy blinked up at the child with deep chocolate brown eyes, as if she was absorbing every word. Grace was thrilled to see that the two were already forging a strong bond with each other.

Although she was shy at first, the puppy soon began to explore the apartment. It didn't take long to realize the little dog needed constant supervision. Her natural curiosity and tendency to chew on things did not make a good combination.

Just as the animal was getting ready to chomp down on the living room lamp's plugged-in cord, Grace scooped her up and said to Clover, "Let's take this ornery little thing for a walk. I think it would be a good idea to burn off some of her excess energy."

Clover thought that was a great idea and bounded over to cradle the dog in her arms. It warmed Grace's heart to see her daughter being such a loving and caring big sister, but she knew they shouldn't coddle the puppy too much.

"I think the puppy needs to walk, rather than be carried," Grace gently informed her daughter. At Clover's crestfallen look, she added, "Dogs like to take in the smells around them and explore. Besides, soon she'll be way too big for you to carry."

At that, Clover's eyes widened to almost double their normal size. "Really?" It was obvious the little girl hadn't had any idea how big Golden Retrievers got. Grace wondered if they might have jumped into this decision a little too quickly as her daughter ran to get the leash from their basket of puppy supplies.

Almost as soon as they reached the sidewalk, it became clear that the puppy was not a fan of being tethered to the leash. She turned around and chomped her sharp teeth on the purple nylon, but she was no match for the thick fabric. They tried to walk a few feet, but it was difficult with the dog whirled around attacking the leash.

Deciding to be firm but kind, Grace bent to take the leash out of the animal's mouth and said, "No."

Both little ones stared up at her with shocked expressions. She rarely had to reprimand Clover, and the dog had obviously never been spoken to with a stern voice. Their stunned gazes almost made Grace chuckle, but she remained strong.

"We need to show her we are the leaders of the pack," Grace told her daughter confidently. "She'll grow into a well-behaved dog if she has clear guidelines to follow."

She had no idea if her words were true, but they sounded good, so she went with it. One thing parenting had taught her was that even though you don't always have all the answers, you fake it until you make it. She made mistakes along the way, but she tried to learn from them and move on. There was no denying she had done a fantastic job so far raising Clover, so she would use the same philosophy with the puppy.

When they resumed their walk, Grace was surprised to see that the puppy left her leash alone. Instead, she flounced from one exciting new odor to the next. The puppy paused to smell grass, mailboxes, trees, light posts, car wheels, and anything else within the range of her leash.

Grace was uncertain what to do when they rounded a corner and came face to face with an incredibly large black dog. The huge, furry animal looked like it must weigh well over a hundred pounds, and there was a long, gleaming goober hanging from its jowl.

The animal seemed friendly enough as it wagged its tail and bent down to sniff the puppy, but Grace and Clover both reared back almost involuntarily. The giant dog looked big enough to swallow their sweet puppy in one bite.

Not having enough sense to be frightened, the puppy's tail was flapping excitedly as she sniffed the enormous creature. She didn't seem to realize that she was only about a tenth of the other animal's size.

The man attempted rather unsuccessfully to restrain the big dog from the other end of leash. At their matching mother and daughter looks of concern and fear, he reassured them. "Not to worry." Grace noticed a faint British accent in his voice. "Newfies are called gentle giants for a reason. My sweet boy, Tiny, is a big teddy bear."

"Your dog's name is Tiny?" Clover bugged her eyes out at the man.

He gave her a friendly smile. "Ironic, isn't it? Do you know what that word means?"

Clover answered, "I think I do now," which made both adults chuckle.

Tiny lifted his head and sniffed the air, evidently catching wind of something more exciting than the puppy. With a great "Woof!" he took off, dragging the surprised man behind him.

Looking down to make sure the puppy was still in one piece, Grace groaned in disgust over the trail of drool on the side of the tiny animal's head. She dug into her purse for some tissues to clean off the slobber.

"Blech! I guess she has now officially been slimed." As usual, Clover lightened the mood and made her mother smile.

When they resumed their walk, Grace noted how almost everyone paused to say a kind word or smile at them. Well, it wasn't really *them*. The puppy seemed to draw out the best in people. Many passersby spoke directly to the dog––telling her how cute she was or how good she was at walking on the leash. The tiny dog preened at their attention, almost as if she could understand what they were saying.

As the trio walked down by the water's edge, they paused to watch some sea lions sunning themselves on the wharf. When one of the animals barked loudly, the puppy jumped in surprise, making both Grace and Clover giggle.

Not to be outdone by the much larger animal, their little dog lifted her head into the air and let out a tiny 'woof' of her own. The sound of her own voice startled her so much that she clumsily fell over on her side.

Grace and Clover couldn't help themselves. They guffawed with laughter at the silly animal. Putting her arm around her daughter, Grace whispered near her ear, "I already love the newest member of our family."

Clover beamed up at her mom. "Really? Me too."

Mother and daughter beamed at each other in a moment of pure happiness. Neither realized what they would soon find out... they had adopted a tiny hurricane.

4

*G*race plopped down onto one of the high stools at Marlene's kitchen counter and blew the hair up off her face. "I'm so tired," she told her landlord, who had morphed into her best friend over the years.

"I can see that." Marlene gave her a warm smile to let her know there wasn't any malice behind her words. After placing a steaming mug of coffee in front of Grace, she sat down beside her.

When Grace rested her face down on her crossed arms on the counter, Marlene reached over to lightly rub her shoulders. The woman's soothing touch felt so good, Grace feared she might fall asleep and drool all over her kind neighbor's counter.

"I don't know how you do it," Grace said into her arms. She didn't have to look up to know Marlene's three children were quietly playing a board game with Clover. Their black lab, Suzie Q, was snoring rather loudly in the corner, and for some inexplicable reason, the puppy was curled up beside her... sound asleep.

Marlene reassured her friend, "I've had years of practice."

Lifting her head, she pointed in the puppy's direction. "She never sleeps like that at home. What are you... the puppy whisperer?"

"She played hard, and now she's resting," Marlene answered logically.

Turning sad eyes on her friend, Grace admitted, "I get so frustrated with her constantly getting into everything she shouldn't that I was beginning to wonder if there is such a thing as shaken puppy syndrome." At her friend's shocked look, she added, "I would never actually do it, but sometimes she is just so exhausting. She's way more work than Clover ever was... even when she was a baby."

"That's why they make puppies so ridiculously cute, so we don't strangle them in frustration," Marlene joked. Softening her expression, she added, "You can't do it all, and you shouldn't even try to. I'm here to help."

"You do it all," Grace pouted, before adding, "And you have way more on your plate than I do." Even though she tried not to compare herself to the other woman, it was difficult not to notice that Marlene made it look so easy to run her bursting-at-the-gills household, while Grace struggled with one child and one overactive puppy.

Marlene reassured her friend, "I have lots of help, and I also have rough days."

Grace had never seen evidence of either of those statements. Marlene's husband, Dan, was the breadwinner of their household, while Marlene took care of everything else. Marlene did it all, and she made it look effortless. Life wasn't a competition, though, and Grace wanted to learn from Marlene's stellar example.

Proving she had some innate sixth-sense about her home's inner workings, Marlene stood and rounded the corner to the oven just before the timer went off. After sliding the homemade oatmeal and chocolate chip cookies onto the cooling rack, she pulled a jug of milk out of the refrigerator and filled four plastic cups for the kids.

After placing a cookie on a napkin in front of Grace, Marlene called the kids in to get their afternoon snack. The children, including Clover, filed in to get their treats, then went to enjoy them at their assigned spots at the table. Clover was an honorary member of their family and had her own designated chair, since Marlene babysat for her when Grace was working at their local grocery's bakery.

Grace marveled at what an impressive and tight ship Marlene ran. Turning to her friend, she said, "I'm so glad you're in my life."

"Me too." Marlene covered Grace's hand with her own in a warm gesture before saying, "Your puppy is starting to stir. We better get her outside before she befouls my carpet."

Grace couldn't imagine how Marlene knew that without looking in the direction of the dogs, but sure enough, the puppy was sniffing around and getting ready to squat. "NO!" she shouted, startling the little dog enough that she froze in her movement.

Running to pick up the dog, Grace yelled, "Wait, wait, please wait," as she scurried to get the puppy outside. When they made it and the puppy squatted in the grass, she praised the animal. "That's a good girl! You are such a good baby!"

She could hear the kids inside the house cackling at her sing-songy dog-mom voice, but she didn't care. She would get the hang of this puppy business because she didn't have any other choice. This little dog was already too important to Clover to give up on it now, so she would figure out how to make it work. She simply had to.

$\mathcal{T}$he next day when Grace ended her shift at the bakery, she went directly to Marlene's house to pick up Clover and the puppy. It was her habit to go there, even before stopping by her own house to change out of her work uniform because she wanted to spend every moment with them that she could.

"Can we take the puppy to the park?' Clover asked excitedly as soon as Grace walked in.

Glancing out the window and realizing it was sunny, despite the brisk breeze, Grace made a snap decision to agree. "That sounds like a great idea." She smiled down at her daughter, making the child beam.

After thanking Marlene and gathering their belongings, Grace started towards the door. Clover already had the puppy leashed, and the animal bounced along happily beside the little girl.

Before the door closed behind them, Marlene called out, "Today would be the perfect day to come up with a name for that little squirt."

Grace sighed as she worked her key into the door on her

side of the house. She knew they needed to name the dog, but finding the perfect moniker seemed like so much pressure. Every name they came up with just didn't seem quite right. It wasn't for a lack of trying, though. She and Clover had been randomly shouting out names at each other for days, but they hadn't yet landed on anything they both agreed was the one.

Once she was changed into stretchy black yoga pants, a soft gray cotton long-sleeved tee shirt and her hot pink tennis shoes, she rejoined her girls in the living room. Grabbing a black fleecy jacket to help ward off the chilly wind, she said to Clover, "Ready to go?"

It was mostly a rhetorical question because the little girl was always ready to go to the park––no matter what the weather was like. Clover said, "Yep!" before running to the door with the puppy hot on her heels.

"Let's make a deal." Grace leaned down to peer right into her daughter's adorable, freckly face.

"What?" Clover's eyes sparkled with anticipation as she gazed up at her Mom.

Grace wondered if she was setting them up for failure, but she was in too far to turn back now. "Let's agree not to come home until we have picked a name for the puppy."

She noticed the wave of concern wash over her daughter's face before the little girl nodded her agreement to Grace's plan.

"Hopefully we won't have to live full-time at the park now." Grace grinned down at her, trying to reassure her daughter that they would land on the perfect name.

Quickly catching on to her mom's humor, Clover added, "Yeah, I love going to the park, but I eventually want to come home."

"You do?" Grace feigned shock. "When exactly does that happen? Because I've never seen you want to come home from the park." She lightly tickled Clover's side, making the child giggle with glee.

The trio happily walked along the sidewalks toward the waterside park where they liked to play. Passersby smiled at the puppy, then Clover, and finally at Grace. They must have made a cute picture because people's faces almost always visibly brightened after seeing them.

As they strolled, Grace and Clover lapsed into their latest game of suggesting and shooting down puppy names.

"What about Princess?" Clover asked, turning her hope-filled gaze up at her mother.

Grace smiled down at her daughter. "I'm fine with it, if that's what you really want, but did you see her the other day after she dug in the mud in the backyard? She hardly looked like Princess material," Grace chuckled.

"That's true," Clover agreed.

Not wanting to shoot down her idea without proposing one of her own, Grace suggested, "How about Sunshine?" She infused her voice with enthusiasm because she favored this option.

"Yeah, that's nice," Clover said, obviously not in love with the name. "We could call her Leaf because she loved chasing that leaf around the other day. Besides, that kind of goes with my name!"

Grace didn't like the idea at all, but she didn't want to discourage her daughter, so she said noncommittally, "Let's keep it on the list of possibilities." Deciding to run with Clover's train of thought, Grace teased, "Maybe she could be Bouncy Red Ball, in honor of the toy she loves more than anything."

"Mo-mmm." Clover rolled her eyes at Grace's lame joke. The glimpse of early pre-teen attitude made Grace's heart flip-flop. Her little girl was growing up way too fast.

"Let's put the search for names completely out of our

minds for a little bit," she suggested, deciding they were over-thinking the name selection. "Maybe the perfect name will just come to us."

"You think so?" Clover looked hopeful.

Grace nodded, hoping she wasn't setting them up for disappointment.

When they arrived at the park, the puppy pounced on a leaf that was fluttering past. Clover gave her mother a clear 'I told you so' look, but before she could say anything, a man in a tailored suit walked up to them.

"What a gorgeous animal!" he practically gushed.

"Thanks!" Clover gave him her best gap-toothed grin, obviously thrilled by his praise of her pet.

Grace felt more cautious about the smooth-talking stranger. She nodded in a friendly manner, but tried to veer their little trio away from the man.

"I don't mean to frighten you," the man assured Grace, sensing her hesitation, "But this puppy is truly remarkable."

"Thanks. Have a nice day." Grace tried to cut him off, feeling even more uncomfortable after his attempt at reassurance.

"Wait," the man pleaded. "I know this sounds crazy, but I need that dog."

Clover sucked in a deep breath and stepped back. She turned her wide gaze up at the man, as if she couldn't quite believe her ears.

"No," Grace told him firmly, before fully turning her family away from the man. Her eyes scanned the park, hoping to find a police officer or security guard.

"I'll pay you," he offered frantically, losing a big chunk of his slick confidence.

Grace quickly maneuvered her girls in the opposite direction of the desperate-sounding man. She fervently hoped he wouldn't follow them.

When he shouted behind them, "I'll give you $10,000 cash for it!" Grace's steps faltered. There was no way she was going to sell him the puppy, and she was fairly certain this was some kind of scam, but that was so much money. It would be a life-changing sum for her.

One glance down at her panic-stricken daughter's face strengthened her resolve. It wouldn't matter if the man offered her a million dollars for the naughty little dog, she couldn't--and wouldn't--do that to Clover.

Shaking her head and continuing their walk without turning back to the crazed man, Grace was annoyed and a bit frightened to hear him hurrying after them. Summoning her courage and resolve, she whirled around to face him. "Look, Mister... The dog is NOT for sale."

"Are you harassing beautiful women in the park, Miles?" The words came from a second man. Grace hadn't realized anyone else had joined the lunatic.

It took a millisecond for her to recognize the gorgeous man she watched on *Good Morning Gold Coast* every morning on the bakery's tiny television while she rolled out dough. When he flashed his megawatt smile in Grace's direction, she had no doubt that she was looking at locally-famous talk show host Dash Diamond.

Grace opened and closed her mouth a few times, probably looking like a carp out of water. She was both stunned and dazzled by the celebrity's sudden appearance. Dash's smile was even brighter in person. It left her completely speechless and a little breathless.

Her daughter, on the other hand, was not at all impressed. Grace was horrified when Clover shook her tiny finger at the men. "Go away! You can't have our puppy." Then the little girl kicked handsome and famous Dash Diamond right in the shin!

6

*D*ash Diamond doubled over and grabbed his injured leg. When he regained his wits enough to look at the little girl before him, his eyes looked as shocked and horrified as Grace's, except his had a trace of fury thrown into the mix.

A frazzled looking woman with a headset and clipboard ran up to the group. Quickly assessing the situation, she whirled on Grace. "What happened?" Accusation dripped from her tone.

"That brat just kicked Dash Diamond!" The stunned celebrity pointed his finger at Clover.

Grace recoiled both at the famous man calling her sweet child a 'brat' and his egotistical reference to himself in the third person. The charming, charismatic talk show host was obviously a pompous jerk in real life.

Knowing her child shouldn't have lashed out physically, but infuriated by his snap judgment, Grace snarled at Dash. "She felt like she had to defend us because your crazy friend was trying to buy our puppy."

Obviously not willing to forgive and forget, Dash whined, "Why did she have to kick me? That's going to leave a bruise."

"She's sorry for hurting you." Grace turned to the child with a firm, "Aren't you?" The little girl nodded, looking down at the ground, obviously on the verge of bursting into tears over the ordeal.

Dash ignored the two of them and turned instead to the production assistant, who seemed to be the most sympathetic about his injury. "Do you think I have any broken bones, Evelyn? Should we go to Gold Coast General Hospital for x-rays?" He lifted the leg of his dark gray suit pants so she could inspect the area.

Evelyn fluttered her lashes, obviously thrilled to be the center of Dash's attention. She peered down, as if she were truly looking for broken bones. "No, I don't think anything is broken," she weighed in. When his expression fell, she quickly added, "Maybe just a sprain."

"Oh, for Pete's sake," Grace huffed, having seen and heard enough. "Nothing is sprained or broken. You might get a bit of a bruise, but nothing too bad--she's just a little girl." Trying to tamp down her temper, but failing, she added, "The biggest bruise is probably to your ego, but yours is so huge I doubt you'll notice."

Dash glared at her before turning to get more coddling from Evelyn. "Do we have a first aid kit at the studio? I think this might need to be wrapped in an Ace bandage."

After Evelyn's nod, he lowered his pant leg and grabbed the assistant's elbow to steady him as he hopped on his good leg. The flustered woman's cheeks turned bright pink as she supported Dash.

Grace couldn't believe what had just happened. Shaking her head to clear it, she mumbled just loud enough for the supposedly-hobbled man to hear, "What a diva."

Whirling around and putting his weight on his 'bad' leg,

Dash's startlingly blue eyes flashed in her direction. "Did you just call me a diva?!? I hate that word. It should be reserved for women. I am NOT a diva."

Grace could tell she had struck a sensitive nerve with him--even more so than her daughter's swift kick to his shin. Normally, she wasn't one to engage in conflict, but this man had her fired up beyond reason. Lifting a brow at him, she said slyly, "If the diva crown fits…"

Dash's eyes filled with fury, and Grace could tell her zinger had hit its mark. He blustered for a moment, searching for a comeback. Evidently coming up empty, he looked down at Evelyn. "Get me out of here," he ordered.

The woman happily complied, obviously thrilled to have Dash leaning on her for support as they turned back towards the road.

Grace stared after them, not quite able to register the sight of the famous man fake-gimping his way out of the park.

When Miles spoke, she jumped slightly because she had forgotten the slick-talking producer was still standing with them. "I've never seen Dash Diamond have such a strong reaction to anyone." He didn't bother to hide the awe in his voice.

"Well, leave it to me to be the first woman he instantly hated," Grace quipped.

"Oh, the energy between you two was electric all right, but I don't think that was truly hate," the producer weighed in with his opinion.

"Sure felt like it," Grace said, taking Clover's hand and turning to leave.

"Wait!" Miles pleaded, making Grace's spine stiffen as she wondered if the smarmy man was going to try to buy her puppy again. "Your brand of chemistry with Dash is exactly what our show needs."

Although Grace was oddly flattered by his assessment, she knew there was no way she could do a talk show. She wanted to shut this idea down before it took root, so she turned back to him to say, "I'm not talk-show host material. Final answer." She looked him directly in the eyes so he would know this wasn't open for discussion. She was too private of a person, and too much of a natural introvert to be a public personality.

Evidently sensing her sincerity, Miles changed gears. "The dog, then?" he asked desperately.

Having had her fill of this conversation, Grace told him in no uncertain terms, "The puppy is NOT for sale... not now, and not ever!"

"Oh, you can keep her," he quickly clarified. "I was thinking maybe she could be a show mascot. She has the looks for television, and it will infuriate Dash to have to share the limelight with her."

Grace figured out the man's motive then. He wanted to ruffle Dash's feathers. As much as the celebrity had annoyed Grace with his over-the-top behavior, she wanted no part of a plan to mess with the man's career. "I don't think so," she brushed off the offer.

"It's only an hour a day," the desperate man tried. Giving her the full-court press, he added, "We'll pay her generously, and we'll hire a trainer to work with her on set." Grace couldn't deny that the extra money would be nice, but she didn't want to live off her dog. That wasn't the way things were supposed to work.

"A dog trainer would be helpful," she said noncommittally.

"Just bring her in for a test screening. You don't have to agree to anything right now." The man bent down to pet the puppy. "She truly has a special look. The audience will love her." He aimed his words at Clover, who smiled back at him--evidently having gotten over her initial wariness.

The puppy sat still, like a regal queen, as the producer fawned over her. Bending down to get an even closer look at her, he asked, "What is this white patch of fur on her chest?" He looked up at them, and then back down at the puppy. "Is it in the shape of a star?" Unable to contain the excitement in his voice, he said, "This is clearly a sign. She is meant to be a star."

Grace and Clover turned to face each other as they fully processed his words. Their mother-daughter connection was in full alignment as they smiled at each other and said the name simultaneously. "Star!"

7

*G*race promised to bring the puppy in for a trial run, but made it clear that if things didn't go well, they would not be continuing with the show.

Miles seemed thrilled to have secured that much of a commitment from her. He gave her the location and timing details, and then quickly slipped away––before she could change her mind.

Trying out the little dog's name for the first time, Clover took a step towards home. Purposely inserting extra enthusiasm into her voice, she said, "Come on, Star!"

Mother and daughter grinned at each other when the little dog stood and followed after her. It was too soon for the animal to know her new name, but it sure seemed like she was already responding to it.

When Clover asked if they could stop by Marlene's house to let the woman know the puppy's name, Grace quickly agreed. During their walk towards home, the doubts had set in about putting Star on television––even for an hour. Marlene was Grace's rock and voice of reason, so she wanted to get her friend's opinion about what had just transpired.

Marlene fawned appropriately over Star's name when Clover burst into her house to reveal it to her. Thrilled by her reaction, the child and puppy ran off to join whatever game Marlene's kids were currently playing.

As soon as she finished recapping the entire scene for her friend, Grace took a bite of her second delicious oatmeal and chocolate chip cookie of the day. It took Marlene a moment to absorb all that she had just been told. Grace wasn't surprised by the slight delay. After all, it wasn't an every day occurrence for her to meet a celebrity or receive offers for her dog to be a talk-show mascot.

Marlene shook her head as it all sank in. "Wow, that's fantastic," she finally weighed in, making Grace sag in relief that she hadn't just made an enormous error in judgment.

As Grace had known she would, Marlene had some sage words of wisdom. "You know, I've always heard having a job boosts a dog's self-esteem. It makes them feel pivotal to the wellbeing of their pack."

Grace hadn't even thought about how the acting job might improve her puppy's socialization and confidence. She had been more worried she was doing something that would in some way harm the animal.

She smiled at Marlene. She was so grateful to have the wise, practical woman in her life. It was so wonderful to have someone to lean on, who was always on her side. Somehow, five minutes with Marlene had already calmed her escalating nerves and made her feel better about her decision to let Star do a tryout on the show.

"Thank you," she told her best friend and confidant sincerely.

Rounding the counter for a warm hug, Marlene said, "Anytime."

Grace called for Clover and chuckled when the little girl came running with the puppy pattering clumsily behind her.

Star's big, fluffy ears bounced as she ran to catch up with her sister.

After giving Clover a goodbye hug, Marlene said, "I hear Star is going to be to be a star!"

The child nodded happily before racing out the back door to the smaller side of the clapboard duplex.

"Let me know how it goes," Marlene called after them as Grace followed her child and puppy home.

Grace promised to do just that before adding, "I just hope she doesn't turn into as big of a diva as Dash Diamond."

She could hear Marlene chuckling behind her when she rounded the corner into her own house and noticed Star staring intently at something. The dog let out a tiny bark, but then looked around the room as if to say, "Who did that?"

Smiling at the silly animal, Grace went over to investigate. She was horrified to discover a great big spider creeping along the living room wall.

Terrified, she sucked in about half the air in the room. Although Grace prided herself on being an independent single mom, spiders gave her the heebie-jeebies.

Used to her mom's panic over the eight-legged creatures, Clover came over and asked, "Where is it?"

Grace was frozen in place, staring in fright at the spider. She managed to raise her arm to point at the wall where the spider had taken up residence. Star woofed again as the creature skittered along the wall.

Clover calmly went to the kitchen and returned with a paper towel. The little girl proceeded to gently scoop the black, hairy spider off the wall and gently wadded the paper towel around it––careful not to hurt the creature.

When she carried the ball past her mother, Grace leaned back out of the way, as if the spider's fangs might shoot out at her. After releasing the spider outside, Clover came back inside with the empty paper towel.

"It's okay, Mama. The spider is gone," Clover sweetly reassured her.

Finally able to breathe normally again, Grace smiled down at her brave, kind child. "What would I do without you?" she wondered aloud, ashamed that her arachnophobia made her freeze up so much that her little girl had to deal with any spiders that entered the perimeter of their house. It had happened enough over the years that they both knew how it needed to be handled.

"And Star," the little girl reminded her. "She found it and pointed it out." Turning to the puppy, she added, "You're a great guard dog, aren't you?"

Grace smiled with pride as she watched her little girl interact with the golden furball. "She's our brave little guard dog," Grace weighed in, agreeing with her daughter's assessment.

Evidently having had her fill of their praise, Star flopped over on her back and began chewing on her own front paw.

"Maybe she needs just a bit more practice at being ferocious," Grace joked as she joined them on the floor and began rubbing the puppy's soft, white belly.

Turning serious, Grace looked at her daughter and said, "I'm supposed to be the one taking care of you two––not the other way around."

"You do take good care of us, Mommy." Clover gazed up at her with huge, adoring eyes. "You're the best Mommy in the whole wide world in the history of forever," the little girl gushed.

Grace noticed the moment the streak of mischief entered the child's eyes, and she knew something else was coming.

"As long as there aren't any spiders involved," Clover added, grinning up at her.

Reaching over, Grace lightly tickled Clover's side, making the child chuckle. Star rolled happily on her back, taking part in the fun. Once their hilarity calmed, the trio rested on their backs on the floor for a moment, all snuggled together.

It was a perfect, happy snapshot in time, and Grace took a moment to savor it. They were now officially a family of three.

Unable to let the calmness last, Star's eyes locked onto the shine of Grace's long silver necklace. Grace noticed, but didn't have time to react before the dog's razor-sharp puppy teeth clamped around the chain.

"It was a perfect moment while it lasted," Grace joked as she tried to gently extricate the rambunctious puppy from her necklace. Locking down her teeth and clearly wanting to play tug-of-war with Grace's inexpensive jewelry, Star let out a tiny growl.

"Hey, I didn't mean you should be ferocious with me!" Grace lightly chastised the puppy. The animal looked so cute--even when she was being naughty--it was impossible to be angry with her.

After finally wrestling the necklace free from the puppy's clamped teeth by distracting her with a squeaky toy, Grace breathed a sigh of relief. "Phew, I feel sorry for any criminal that decides to cross our guard dog," she told Clover.

When they went to bed, Star loped along behind Clover as if she knew the routine and that her place was by the little girl's side. Grace smiled when she went to tuck her daughter into bed and realized that Star was snuggled right up against Clover and already lightly snoring.

Grace climbed into her own bed, confident she had made the right decision bringing the ornery, adorable little puppy into their lives. She couldn't have imagined the extreme highs and devastating lows of being a puppy mom that were yet to come.

8

*S*tar's big television debut day quickly arrived, and Grace was nervous. She knew it was silly to be apprehensive for her pet, but she couldn't help it. At least it wasn't going to be her in front of the cameras. That would probably give her a nervous breakdown.

Grace had arranged to take the day off work from the grocery bakery, and she let Clover miss the day from school, so they could both be there for Star's big moment. After all, it wasn't every day that a family member became famous.

She was guessing Star's appearance on the show would be a one-time deal because she couldn't imagine they would want a rambunctious and unpredictable puppy on a live television program, so she wanted their little family to enjoy every moment of Star's 'fifteen minutes of fame.'

As they walked to the studio early on the morning of the show, Grace joked with Clover. "We should enjoy this peaceful walk because after this morning, Star will be a celebrity who gets recognized and hounded for autographs everywhere she goes."

Grace knew her 'hounded' wording went right over

Clover's head, but the little girl grinned up at her anyway. "You think so?" The enthusiasm was unmistakable in the child's voice.

Not wanting to set her daughter up for disappointment, Grace toned it down a bit. "I bet at least one person will recognize her," she predicted.

Unfazed by the downgrade, Clover said, "Cool!" and jumped in the air. Evidently having an idea mid-leap, she whirled on her mom. "We might need to change her name to Super Star!"

Grace couldn't help but smile at Clover's excitement. "Maybe," she agreed noncommittally, not wanting to dampen the child's enthusiasm.

When they arrived at the studio, they were quickly ushered inside. Grace recognized Miles and Evelyn as two of the many people who were bustling around doing show prep.

A man she hadn't met presented her with a clipboard full of waivers and releases to sign. "I feel like I'm signing my puppy's life away," she tried to joke with him, but he didn't crack a smile.

As soon as she finished the paperwork, he quickly vanished and a peppy young woman with a high, bouncy ponytail appeared before them. She leaned down to greet Star. "Aren't you a beauty? I'm Nora, the set dog trainer." Her introduction was obviously aimed at Grace and Clover, but she never managed to tear her eyes away from Star.

The puppy lolled on her back, enjoying the undivided attention as Nora rubbed her fluffy belly.

"I'll take good care of her," Nora promised, still gazing at the dog. With that, she stood and said, "Come on, Star! Let's go get you camera-ready."

The puppy loped happily after the trainer, without a backward glance at her family. Grace and Clover were left standing alone in the whirling activity of the studio, wondering what they were supposed to do.

They eventually caught Evelyn's eye. She rushed over to them, even as she was scribbling frantically on her clipboard and speaking into her headset. Once she was in front of them, she made eye contact with Grace and asked, "Are you ready?"

Glad to have someone to guide them, Grace answered, "Oh, yes. We are so excited for today. We've been working with Star and having her practice…"

Grace's answer was interrupted by Evelyn's pointer finger being raised in her direction, effectively shushing her. "What was that? Someone here was talking right in my face. How long before you're ready?"

Feeling stunned and a little miffed, Grace stared at the abrasive woman as she continued her conversation with the person on the other end of her headset. Unsure what to do other than stand and wait for her to finish her conversation, Grace peeked down and raised one eyebrow at Clover in their unspoken mother-daughter version of relaying that she couldn't believe the gall of the woman in front of them. Clover nodded in agreement, understanding what Grace was trying to tell her.

It dawned on Grace then that Evelyn had just repeated the same words twice. Returning her gaze to the woman, who was tapping her foot with impatience, Grace asked, "What was that?"

Speaking slowly, as if Grace were completely dense, Evelyn said, "Are you ready to go sit down?"

"Oh, I didn't realize you were speaking to us this time." Grace defended her failure to respond earlier. When the other woman rolled her eyes, Grace bit her tongue, refusing to let the woman's impatience and rudeness rile her or ruin this day. She gave her a brisk nod in answer to the question.

Evelyn whirled away, without another word, so Grace assumed they were supposed to follow her. She was pleased when the woman ushered them to two chairs, which had been set up on the side of the stage. It would be an angled view of the action, but they didn't have the cameras blocking their line of sight like the regular audience did.

Tapping her foot impatiently, Evelyn waited for them to make their way over the cords and other tripping hazards to their seats. "That's an interesting shirt." It was the first remotely kind words the woman had uttered to Grace.

"Oh, thanks!" Grace looked down and brushed a hand over her top. She'd spent an inordinate amount of time choosing what to wear this morning.

Rather than saying 'you're welcome,' like any normal human being would, Evelyn responded, "I got my mom that nightgown one year for her birthday."

Grace tried not to let the humiliation show on her face. She had thought the oversized black shirt with bright pink peonies looked fantastic over her leggings. It had never dawned on her that the big tee might actually be a nightshirt.

Evelyn hurried away without any further insults. Grace couldn't help but wonder if the hateful woman would tell Dash Diamond about Grace's fashion faux pas. She could clearly imagine the two of them sharing a laugh at her expense.

Grace tried not to feel too self-conscious about apparently wearing pajamas to the show as she and Clover settled themselves into their chairs. Clover looked around to make sure Evelyn was no longer within hearing range before saying near her mother's ear, "I think that woman is appropriately named."

Unsure what her daughter was getting at, Grace asked, "Oh?"

Clover nodded, obviously proud of whatever she was

going to say next. Tipping up closer to whisper, so she wouldn't be overheard, Clover said, "Evil-lyn."

Grace couldn't stop the giggle that erupted out of her at her child's wit––even though it was a little mean-spirited. Once she had that initial uncensored reaction under control, she gave the little girl a firm warning by saying, "That's not kind." She didn't want to encourage her daughter to say such things because they tried to always live by the golden rule. She didn't get too angry about it, though, because the woman *had* proven herself to be quite rude.

Looking around at the studio, Grace was surprised by how small it was. It seemed much bigger when she watched the show on television. She didn't have long to marvel at the magic of television optical illusions because an announcer came out to pump up the crowd. Before long, he had them clapping, laughing, and clamoring to see the one and only Dash Diamond.

Due to the positioning of their chairs, Grace was able to catch a glimpse of Dash as he appeared at the side-stage entrance. He had what looked like paper napkins tucked into the snow-white collar of his dress shirt, and a woman was scrambling behind him, attempting to powder away any hint of face shine.

He was quite obviously agitated as he barked into his cell phone. "When I said any dumb blonde could sit beside me, I didn't mean THIS!" He sounded outraged, just before he jabbed his finger on the screen to end the call.

Grace had expected he wouldn't be pleased to find out he was sharing the stage with her puppy, but she had assumed he would react better than this. In his defense, from his enraged tone, it sounded like he had just found out about Star's appearance on the show. He should have been told before now, but perhaps his handlers had anticipated his childish overreaction. She just hoped he wouldn't ruin Star's big moment.

On queue, the announcer revealed to the audience that they were here on a very special day because the search for Dash's next co-host had gone to the dogs... literally. His voice overflowed with enthusiasm as it boomed, "Say hello to the Gold Coast's most adorable puppy... Star!"

The crowd went wild––clapping, whistling, and yelling. Nora trotted Star out on her leash. The puppy pranced, almost like she knew they were all cheering for her. Once Nora had Star settled on the sofa with a toy to chew on, the woman moved behind the couch and crouched down out of the view of the camera. She evidently intended to stay there during the live show to handle any puppy issues. That knowledge made Grace breathe a little easier.

When she noticed the glittering collar around Star's neck, she leaned forward to get a better look at it. The viewing monitor gave her a better view of the star-shaped pendant that was engraved with the puppy's name. Leaning down to whisper in her daughter's ear, she asked, "Are those diamonds on Star's tag?"

Clover looked and decided, "They sure look like diamonds."

Grace rolled her eyes. "I hope they don't turn her into as big of a prima donna as Dash Diamond." Her hushed words made Clover giggle.

As if her mentioning his name summoned him, Dash left his spot where he had been waiting in the wings and strolled confidently in front of them. The makeup lady ripped the paper protection from around his neck just as the announcer said, "And without further adieu, here is the man of the hour... Dash Diamond!" He drew out Dash's last name for at least three seconds.

With perfect timing, Dash donned his electric smile and

waved to his adoring fans. "Hello, everyone. Thank you for being here. I hope you enjoy the show."

A man, who Grace assumed was the director, yelled frantically, "Ten seconds to show time! Places, everyone!"

Proving he had been through this many times before, Dash remained unfazed by the man's panicked tone. "I guess that means me," he said jovially before strolling calmly over to the couch where Star was happily chewing on her toy.

Grace briefly wondered if they had some kind of catnip for dogs on that toy because she had never seen Star sit so still and be so calm for so long. She had thought Marlene had serious puppy mojo, but Nora must truly be the puppy whisperer.

With perfect timing, Dash sat down on the sofa and flashed his signature smile. The director pointed to him, indicating the silent part of the countdown was over, and the hushed audience waited with bated breath for him to speak.

"*Good Morning Gold Coast*," Dash said in his deep, yet friendly, television voice. When he was on camera, he somehow managed to find the perfect blend of enthusiasm and approachability––without seeming fake. Grace almost wished she hadn't ever encountered the man in real-life, so she could continue to believe his on-air persona was real.

Dash introduced Star as his beautiful, smart, and lovable co-host for the day. If Grace hadn't seen his reaction to the puppy five minutes ago, she would have believed he was being sincere.

The man who had pumped up the audience earlier waved his hands for them to clap, and the crowd went wild for Star. The puppy startled at the sudden noise––after the relative quiet.

It all happened so fast, Grace barely had time to register her humiliation. She and Nora realized at the same time what was about to happen, but they were both too late to stop it. The puppy circled around and sniffed at the area, then the animal squatted to relieve herself on the set's fancy sofa cushion on live television!

As soon as Dash saw the liquid circle spreading, his eyes darted straight to Grace, and they were filled with fury.

9

The audience stared in stunned silence. Proving that he was a consummate professional who could handle any curveball live television might throw in his direction, Dash quickly regained his wits.

Turning to look directly into the camera, he deadpanned, "Well, I've had my fair share of nervous co-hosts before, but this is the first time THAT happened."

One dazzling signature smile later, the crowd was chuckling. Nora efficiently moved Star to Dash's other side. The cameras reset their angles. The soiled sofa cushion was whisked away, miraculously replaced with a clean one, and the show quickly moved on from the awkward moment.

Dash seamlessly steered the show. It was a well-known fact in Redwood Cove that he struggled to find a suitable co-host. Half of the starlets in Hollywood had tried to join him on the program, but they never seemed to last more than a few days. It had never dawned on Grace before meeting the man that it might be *his* fault that his co-stars never worked out. His charming onscreen persona was apparently just an act.

Through Dash's knack for effortless flirtation with the camera, he was easily able to host the show by himself, but that didn't stop the producers from constantly searching for his new co-host. After this morning's fiasco with Star's appearance, Grace was certain they wouldn't feel any closer to finding the right female to sit by his side.

When she noticed Clover shivering, Grace retrieved the light sweater she had brought in her oversized purse to wrap around the girl's shoulders. The studio was surprisingly chilly.

Grace tried not to feel too embarrassed when Star kept attempting to climb onto Dash's lap while they were on the air. They had to have known what they were getting into when they invited the young animal on the show, right?

The celebrity host never skipped a beat as he kindly, but firmly set Star aside over and over again. The stubborn little animal decided they were playing a game and made it her sole mission in life to pounce on, nip at, and otherwise terrorize Dash as he did his best to ignore her roughhousing.

The studio audience was enthralled with the ornery puppy and her interaction with the unflappable host of the show. They smiled and chuckled at each of her antics as Dash talked, joked, and entertained them as if nothing were amiss. He was obviously the type of professional television personality who could calmly report the news from the eye of a hurricane. In fact, he already was... this particular hurricane was named Star.

During the first commercial break, Dash stood and walked towards the side door from where he had entered earlier. He was back on his cell phone and, by the flailing of his arms, Grace deduced that he was incredibly agitated.

She could hear snippets of his conversation. "...you see that?...absolute travesty... won't put up with it..."

It was her guess that she, Clover, and Star were about to

be escorted out of the building by security. When that didn't happen, she was truly surprised.

The producers of the show must have been incredibly determined to keep Star on for the duration of the hour-long program because Nora reappeared and plopped the puppy down on the couch—just as Dash sauntered over and turned his camera charm back on to resume the show.

As Grace watched him, she decided there was no denying that Dash Diamond had an abundance of charisma. It was too bad she now knew what a pompous jerk he was in real life.

When Dash announced the first guest on the show, Jessie Black, the crowd clapped appropriately for the arrival of the Hollywood has-been. A few years ago, Jessie had been in high-demand for every action hero role, but after what was supposed to be a huge summer blockbuster turned into a gigantic flop, he couldn't seem to make a movie work.

Jessie almost seemed desperate when he turned to the camera and asked the audience to go see his latest movie. When he made a joke about having to feed his kids, it fell completely flat.

The awkward silence seemed like it was going to drag on a bit too long when Star suddenly pounced. She leaped right over Dash, who had been gently shoving her back into her spot whenever she tried to make her way to Jessie. Evidently having had enough of his restraint and desperate to meet Jessie, she landed directly in the star's lap.

The sudden appearance of the puppy startled Jessie, but he quickly recovered. Beaming a sincere smile at the animal, he held her up and nuzzled his bristly face against her soft fur. "Aren't you the sweetest little thing?" The Southern drawl he had been known for earlier in his career miraculously returned.

His slight twang, along with his cuddling of the adorable

puppy, made for a delightful combination, and the audience warmed to him. Soft "awws" and whispered tittering spread throughout the crowd.

Picking up on the shift, Jessie milked the moment. "How about if you come with me on this press junket, Darlin'?" He spoke directly to the puppy, making the women in the audience practically swoon.

He was really laying it on thick, but Grace had to admit this softer side of Jessie Black was rather attractive. She might even go see his new movie.

The puppy snuggled into Jessie's face, obviously thrilled to have made her way past Dash. Proving that she couldn't be a sweet angel for too long, she chomped down on the fleshy part of Jessie's ear.

Jessie's eyes bulged out and Grace guessed that he was struggling not to cuss on live television. She knew how much the puppy's razor-sharp baby teeth hurt, so she didn't discount the pain the celebrity must have been feeling.

Nora's hand quickly snaked up from behind the couch, while her body remained hidden from the cameras. She efficiently used a squeaky toy to distract the puppy's attention from her lock-down on Jessie's ear.

Jessie rubbed his sore ear lobe between his thumb and finger. "Phew. Those teeth are like little needles." The words were said more to himself than to Dash or the camera.

Ignoring the interruption and smoothly turning the attention back to the interview, Dash prompted, "So, tell us more about your latest movie."

Star plopped down between the two men and started chomping on her squeaky toy. Grace wondered if the puppy trainer had picked the loudest toy in the world when Star began squeaking it at random intervals during Jessie's answer.

"Well, at first glance"--SQUEAK--"it might seem

like"--SQUEAK--"this   fourth"--SQUEAK, SQUEAK--"movie is just another sequel to make us all more money, but I"--SQUEAK--"truly believe movie-goers"-- SQUEAK--"will be pleasantly"--SQUEAK--"surprised by the inventive storyline, thrilling action sequences, and of course the steamy love"--SQUEEEEEEAK--"scenes."

Grace was horrified by Star's behavior, even though the animal was simply acting like what she was... a puppy. Jessie handled the multiple interruptions to his monologue like a true professional--stopping and starting whenever Star's random outbursts allowed.

Dash, however, was beginning to show the first chinks in his unflappable armor. He grabbed the squeaky toy from the surprised puppy and hurled it behind the couch.

"Okay, thank you for your patience with our latest co-host attempt," Dash said to Jessie. "I think it's clear to everyone now that she isn't going to work out."

His anger was barely concealed as his fiery blue eyes flashed at the camera. Star seemed perplexed by how her toy had disappeared, so she began sniffing Dash's hands as if it was somehow hidden in them. Unable to find her toy or figure out where it went, Star plopped her butt down, looked up at Dash, and gave him a tiny and adorable, "Woof!"

The crowd went wild, laughing and clapping for the rambunctious little pup. Everyone in the entire studio was smiling at her antics, with one glaring exception--Dash Diamond.

After smoothly transitioning to commercial break, Dash stood and lifted Star. He held the wriggly puppy out away from his body. "Nora," he snapped, "this thing needs to go... Now."

The in-studio audience immediately turned on the normally-beloved host. There were some shocked inhala-tions and even an unmistakable 'boo.'

Dash looked stunned, but he quickly recovered. "She'll be right back, folks," he promised, gracing them with one of his winning smiles.

When he turned, Grace noticed that Dash's smile immediately fell away. She didn't really like this close backstage look into the show. She had enjoyed believing that Dash was as friendly and charming in real life as he seemed on television. Watching him seem to play a role in front of the crowd was obliterating that fantasy.

Dash went to the side of the stage where he was hidden from the audience, but he was still within Grace and Clover's line of vision. He started rubbing his nose frantically, even as the make-up woman attempted to touch up his powder.

Ignoring her, he batted furiously at his face as if he had just walked through a spider web. Grace heard him growl to no one in particular, "That beast's fur is everywhere!"

Shocked by what he had called her adorable pet, Grace's head whipped back as if she had been slapped. Certain the crowd would turn on Dash for that hateful remark, she turned to gauge their reaction.

The hype man was doing his job of entertaining the audience during the lulls in the action. He had them so pumped up they apparently hadn't heard Dash's outburst.

Grace felt a little disappointment that Dash wouldn't have to face an angry crowd for picking on her innocent pup. She was quickly distracted, though, by the activity on the set.

She watched in horror as they set up the kitchen for a cooking segment. A trickle of optimism made its way in to her mind that maybe they were going to have Star sit out for this portion of the show. That glimmer of hope was quickly dashed when Nora arrived and arranged Star on a cushioned puppy bed right on the counter.

Clover and Grace made eye contact as soon as they realized what was happening. "Oh no," they groaned in unison.

10

*G*race feared Dash might walk off the set right in the middle of the live show when he realized what was happening. He surprised her, though. Other than a slight stutter in his steps toward the makeshift kitchen when he noticed Star's placement on the counter, he gave no external indication that anything was amiss.

She realized he was probably hoping this clip would be a fiasco, so he could convince his producers that any further shows with Star would be a huge mistake.

She decided if that happened to suggest the producers select an older dog to sit alongside Dash as the show's mascot. The crowd obviously loved having a canine on the stage; Star just wasn't mature enough yet to be trusted on live television. She was too unpredictable, but a more mature dog probably wouldn't be. In fact, she might hint that she could bring Star back in a year or two––once she calmed down a little.

Smoothly changing gears back into 'talk-show host' mode, Dash smiled for the camera and introduced his next guest. "Please give a warm welcome to Emily Hart, the Head Chef at Tuck In, the hottest new restaurant in town."

The beautiful woman sashayed in, beaming at the crowd. Emily baby-talked to the puppy and overtly flirted with Dash. They both seemed to soak up and enjoy her attention.

Grace didn't understand the burst of jealousy that flared as she watched the talented, dark-haired beauty charm her puppy and Dash. As much as she didn't want things to go wrong, a small and unfamiliar streak in her wished Star would step in the woman's fancy bowl of fennel and feta gourmet salad.

Not liking this envious side of herself, she shook her head in a futile attempt to physically ward off her negative feelings. The gorgeous chef had every right to be here fawning over her puppy and Dash. It didn't make sense for Grace to be jealous. She loved it when people gushed over her puppy––and she didn't even like full-of-himself Dash Diamond!

What did it matter if Dash struck up a relationship with the lovely chef? It didn't. The unsettled feeling deep in Grace's belly must be nerves that Star was going to get into further mischief before the end of the show.

Speaking of that, Emily and Dash were struggling to keep the stubborn and wily puppy away from the hot burners where Emily was heating homemade zucchini noodles and a red pasta sauce that smelled divine. Both of them gently nudged her away and told her, "No," but Star took their light reprimands as a challenge and stepped up her efforts to get past them to investigate the hot food.

Finally letting a bit of his frustration show, Dash turned his head to look pointedly at someone off-camera. Grace assumed it was the show's director. "How about if the dog isn't included in this segment, since she can't seem to resist trying to burn herself?" His voice sounded cool and rational, but Grace could tell by his flashing eyes that he was livid just beneath the surface of his calm exterior.

"Oh, she's fine." Emily cooed, lifting the little puppy and making kissing noises near her face. She turned Star over and cradled her like a baby before beginning to bark orders at Dash. "Turn the back burner down to low and stir the sauce."

The puppy batted at Emily to regain her attention, so the chef brought Star's paw to her mouth and pretended like she was going to eat it. "Nom, nom, nom." She smiled down at Star.

Dash complied with her requests before turning to gawk at the woman as if seeing her for the first time. He didn't bother to hide his look of disgust over her coddling of Star.

Not giving him a break, Emily said, "The pasta is ready to be drained."

"Oh, let me get it. It's not like we have a famous chef here." Dash said, failing to conceal the sarcasm in his tone.

Grace couldn't understand it, but she was enjoying watching the less-friendly shift in the relationship between the two humans in the studio kitchen.

When Star began to squirm restlessly in the chef's arms, Emily reached over to pluck a breadstick from the glass where they were standing artfully arranged like a bouquet of flowers. When she popped the breadstick into Star's open mouth, the puppy clamped down on the treasure.

Proving that she truly was star material, the pup turned to face the camera with the breadstick poking out on both sides of her mouth. She looked like she was smiling right into the lens. The in-house crowd clapped with delight.

With perfect timing, the segment ended. The flurry of activity on the set resumed as the show went on pause for the final commercial break.

Chef Emily handed off Star to Nora before doing a flirty

finger wave in Dash's direction. Obviously having lost interest in her, Dash lifted his hand to show her his palm. The lack of enthusiasm in his gesture was clear, even from across the stage where Grace was seated.

Dash refrained from making any heated phone calls during this break. Instead, he went out to schmooze the crowd. They hung on his every word as he bantered with them—somehow making them feel special and appreciated, even though he had a new studio audience every day.

Grace marveled at how quickly he was able to turn his charm—and his obvious annoyance—on and off. She had to give him props for being a true professional, especially since she had seen first-hand his anger at having to share the limelight with Star.

Once he had the crowd back in the palm of his hand, he returned to the sofa to close out the show. Nora whisked back in and placed Star right next to Dash's leg. For his part, the celebrity host completely ignored the puppy's presence. It almost seemed like he believed if he didn't acknowledge her, then she wasn't actually there, ruining his morning.

The audience silenced during the countdown. Dash spoke into the camera as he thanked the viewers for watching and asked them to tune in tomorrow. He had an uncanny knack for seeming like he was truly talking to each person individually, even though he was speaking into a camera lens. Grace had experienced his on-air charisma herself when she had the show on at work. He somehow made it feel like he was talking directly to her.

After he made his spiel, he prepared to sign-off the ending segment. Not to be outdone, Star forced her way onto his leg. Dash steadfastly ignored her as he said his signature closing line, "Make it a great day, Gold Coast. I'll see you tomorrow."

Somehow sensing her cue, Star gave a happy little

"Woof!" Her spot-on comedic timing thrilled the crowd, who clapped and whistled enthusiastically as the credits scrolled and the show came to a close.

Grace glanced down at Clover, who had been riveted to the behind-the-scenes activity of the show. The little girl hadn't made a peep during the entire hour. "Did you have fun?" she asked her daughter.

"Oh, yes!" Clover looked up at her. "Star is meant to be a star," she added dreamily.

Grace wasn't sure how to break it to her daughter that this was bound to be a one-time gig. She was certain Dash Diamond wouldn't deign to share the stage with their puppy again.

Saving her from having to formulate the right wording, Dash himself rushed past them, holding his cell phone to his ear and speaking furiously. "Make sure we never have that dog or any other on the show again. This isn't a circus, and I'm done performing with animals," he said with finality.

Even before glancing down, Grace knew her daughter would be heartbroken over the celebrity's harsh words. Sure enough, Clover's eyes were already pooling with tears.

Shaking her head and pulling the sweet child into a hug, Grace silently cursed the full-of-himself celebrity. The only good thing to come out of Star's unceremonious firing was that they would never have to see that pompous, arrogant jerk again.

*E*mbarrassed that her puppy's big television debut had turned into a fiasco and upset that her daughter looked so distraught, Grace hurried over to retrieve Star so they could all get out of the studio and retreat to the healing solace of their home.

Nora was kneeling on the studio floor praising the pup over what a good girl she was and telling her what a wonderful job she did on the show. Star lifted her chin proudly, as if she could understand every word the woman was saying.

Knowing the woman's praise was stretching the truth, and fairly certain that Star couldn't actually understand her, Grace bent to scoop up the puppy.

For her part, Nora looked truly sad to see the animal go. She ruffled Star's soft ears and said in a sing-songy voice, "See you tomorrow, sweet girl."

"Tomorrow?!?" Grace practically spluttered. "I don't think we'll be coming back."

The other woman looked perplexed by Grace's response. "Why ever not? Star did a wonderful job. In fact, she practically stole the show. How can you deny her the ability to show off her natural talent?"

Hearing Dash's booming voice in the distance, Grace waved her hand in his direction and mumbled, "Because she practically stole the show." Despite how much Nora and the studio audience enjoyed Star's antics on the program, Grace knew the actual star of the show had not appreciated her puppy one tiny bit. He was likely arranging to have her little family forcibly removed and banned for life from the studio right now.

"Grace, darling!" Miles sidled up beside her. "What did I tell you?" Without waiting for a response, the producer answered his own question. "This little angel is meant to be a star." He patted Star on the head a little too roughly before turning his attention back to Grace. "Why don't you come upstairs and we'll get her contract squared away?"

Grace couldn't believe her ears. It was obvious the producer hadn't yet spoken with the show's host. As soon as he did, he would surely change his tune. "I think you might want to talk to Dash about that," Grace suggested.

"Oh, he'll come around." Miles sounded confident, but Grace was just as sure Dash wouldn't change his mind about sharing the stage with Star.

"I don't think so," Grace said confidently before turning to get Clover so they could leave.

Panic rose in her throat when she realized the little girl wasn't right beside her. She hadn't felt her leave, even though she was normally completely in sync with the child's movements, as if she had a sixth sense about her whereabouts. "Clover?" she called out, frantically scanning the studio.

The crowd had dispersed, so it was mostly just stage-hands and show staff remaining on the set. Grace struggled to breathe as she looked for her little girl. Still holding Star, she left Miles to go search for Clover. Her heart hammered and her pulse pounded in her head as she raced around looking for her missing daughter. "Has anyone seen a little girl?" she called out in desperation, but no one seemed to pay her any attention.

Just as she was getting ready to screech in panic to get their help, she caught sight of Clover's bright purple tennis shoe. Running over to the side of the stage, relief overwhelmed her when she realized that her daughter was safe and sound.

Grace froze in her tracks when she noticed that the man squatted down to Clover's eye-level, seeming to hang on her every word, was none other than Dash Diamond. She approached slowly, certain the celebrity would bolt away once he realized Clover was with her and Star. He obviously hadn't recognized Clover from their unfortunate encounter in the park.

The little girl was speaking importantly. "My mommy chose to call me Clover because it has the word love right in the middle of my name." The little girl proceeded to spell out her name for the talk-show host, as if he might not comprehend what she meant.

"Well, look at that!" Dash sounded truly impressed. "Your mom must have known you would be special, so she came up with a name that had love built right into it." Obviously not realizing Clover was the girl who kicked his shin, he tweaked her nose, making the little girl beam.

Grace couldn't help but smile at the sweet interaction. She was charmed, despite herself. Too bad Dash couldn't be that kind and agreeable all the time.

Clover nodded enthusiastically. "You can ask her yourself, 'cause here she is now." The little girl pointed up at Grace and Star.

The open, friendly look immediately drained from Dash's face when he realized who she was. "Oh." His voice sounded flat--completely devoid of the enthusiasm it held just moments ago.

"Time to go," Grace said firmly to Clover, hoping to avoid an awkward conversation with Dash.

"Go?" Miles walked up behind her. "But you haven't signed Star's contract yet. I had our lawyers draw up the paperwork during the show, and I'd like to get all of the required signatures in place today."

"Contract?!?" Dash stood to his full height, his face already turning red with anger. "You mean to tell me you are considering letting this... this... brat on my show again?" Dash towered over Miles, obviously intending to intimidate the much shorter man.

Grace's hackles rose. "She's not a brat. She's just a puppy. They are like toddlers, and they get into things. It's what they do."

"Exactly. Which is why they should *not* be featured on live television." Dash made it sound like Grace was making his point for him, even though that hadn't been her intent.

"The approval ratings for Star were through the roof." Miles told Dash, not backing down a bit from the tall man looming over him. "Just look at these preliminary numbers." He held some papers with colorful graphs out towards Dash.

Something on the top page caught Dash's eye, so he swiped the pile from Miles's outstretched hand. Dash flipped quickly through the entire stack of charts and grids, with his expression morphing into one of cautious optimism. When he looked up, his eyes went directly to Star before landing on Miles. "Whoa," he said in his least eloquent statement of the morning.

Seeming to understand what he meant, Miles jumped in. "I know, right? She could single handedly save the show. Well, single pawed-ly." Chuckling at his own joke, Miles looked between Dash, Grace, and Clover to see if they appreciated his humor.

Clover was the only one that looked amused. Grace was too surprised to hear that the show might need saving to laugh. Dash was looking at Star with fresh eyes and what appeared to be a bit of renewed hope.

"I still don't like it," Dash weighed in, his opinion obviously having been somewhat swayed after seeing the ratings.

"You don't have to like it," Miles assured him. "You just have to accept it."

Nodding, Dash said, "It's only an hour a day, right?"

"That's right!" Miles answered enthusiastically, obviously thrilled to have gotten the host on board with his plan. Smiling at the others, he added, "What could go wrong in an hour a day?"

Grace couldn't help but wonder if the producer's glib question held a foreboding of disastrous live television debacles just ahead.

*O*nce the intimidating stack of paperwork was signed, Evelyn briskly ushered Grace and her girls out of the network's four-story building. The woman spoke quickly as she gave Grace instructions about the details of Star's employment.

"She needs to be here every weekday at 7:00 a.m. sharp to be groomed before the show."

"Oh," Grace furrowed her brow as she wondered how she was going to make that happen. That time was right in the middle of her early-morning shift at the bakery. Marlene already made sure Clover and her own kids got to Gold Coast Elementary School every morning. Grace couldn't ask her to be responsible for this, too.

Grace tucked her hair behind her ear as she scrambled to think of a solution. She didn't want to back out of Star's contract, but she couldn't leave work every day to deliver the pup here. Sometimes it really wasn't any fun being a single mom. It would be nice to have a significant other who could help with some of these predicaments.

Seeming to sense Grace's worry, Evelyn asked, "Shall I send a car for her, then?"

Grace almost couldn't believe her ears. Her dog was being offered limousine service?!? What kind of alternative universe had she slipped into? She bugged her eyes out at Evelyn, but the woman appeared to be completely serious.

"Well, if it's not too much trouble, that would be a huge help," Grace admitted.

Nodding, Evelyn scribbled something on her ever-present clipboard. "Consider it done," she responded efficiently.

As they reached the front door, Evelyn handed Grace a paper paycheck. "Here is Star's pay for the day. Now that she's under an annual contract, she'll be paid bi-weekly. You'll need to set up automatic deposit with the payroll department because they don't like cutting physical checks."

Grace stared at the paper in stunned silence. She had been aware that Star would be paid for her on-air time, but this entire scenario seemed utterly surreal.

"Star's limo will arrive at the address we have on file for you tomorrow at 6:30 a.m. Please make sure she is ready to go. Good day," Evelyn added formally, holding the door open and effectively dismissing them out onto the sidewalk.

The trio walked out the door and paused on the sidewalk so Grace could collect her thoughts. Glancing down at the check in her hand, she was amazed to see that it was written for one-thousand dollars. That was more money than she made in an entire week at the bakery.

Grace held the check up for Clover's inspection. The little girl probably wouldn't be able to read the words, but she would see all of those zeroes. "A thousand bucks isn't bad for an hour of work, huh?" She grinned down at her daughter.

"A thousand bucks?" Clover parroted her with her eyes wide open in excitement. "We can buy a rocket ship!"

Grace chuckled at her child's somewhat misguided enthusiasm. "Not quite," she hedged, not wanting to stifle Clover's wild imagination.

They turned towards home and walked in amiable silence for a bit. Grace could tell that Clover was deep in thought about something, so she wasn't surprised when the little girl turned to gaze up at her. "Mommy?"

At Grace's nod, she went on. "Star made a thousand bucks today, even though she slept through part of the show. Imagine how much she'll make if she stays awake the whole time!"

Grace's eyes had nearly popped out of their sockets over Star's official salary on the contract. She knew the puppy was going to be earning huge money on the show––whether she slept or not. She was aware she probably should have had some representation to negotiate better compensation for the puppy before signing, but the entire deal was such a windfall that she hadn't hesitated.

The money Star earned could go directly into a college fund for Clover that would take the pressure off Grace when that time rolled around. It was a big relief to know the money for Clover's education was secured. She had been tucking away a small amount from her bakery paychecks, but Star's earnings would put that meager sum to shame.

She was smiling with relief that Clover would be able to go to whatever educational institution she chose when a woman stopped in front of them.

"Star?" the lady asked, her voice filled with disbelief. She bent down to get a closer look at the puppy. Reaching out, she inspected the bedazzled pendant the studio had placed on the puppy's collar. She scratched Star's nape as she spoke to her. "I can't believe it's really you! I watched you on television this morning, and you did such a good job."

Grace and Clover stood by awkwardly while the woman

fawned over the pup. They weren't quite sure what to say or do. It was a normal event for Star to get smiles or even brief rubdowns from strangers, but this woman obviously recognized Star and seemed to want to have an entire conversation with her.

"Oh, you're even prettier in person than you were on camera," the woman gushed over the preening puppy. Realizing her flub, the woman amended her statement. "I guess you're not actually in person. You're in puppy!" she decided proudly. Her voice took on the sing-songy tone that most people adopted when speaking to Star.

For her part, the puppy relished the attention. She rolled over onto her back in a not-so-subtle hint for the woman to rub her white belly.

Grace was ready to go, but she wasn't sure how to extricate her puppy from the excited lady. The woman was showing no sign of being ready to leave as she obediently scratched Star's belly, while speaking quietly to her.

"We need to get going," Grace finally said.

The woman looked startled, as if she had forgotten anyone else was there. "Oh!" Her eyes suddenly lit up. She dug in her purse before shoving her phone into Grace's hand. "Will you take a picture of me with Star? My friends will be so excited to see that I met her."

"Umm. Sure." Grace took the phone. The lady picked up Star, so Grace snapped a picture. When she went to hand the phone back, the woman refused it and instead asked, "Just a few more poses?"

Without waiting for a response from Grace, she held the puppy aloft in the air as if they were getting ready to smooch. Not one to miss an opportunity like that, Star swiped her wet pink tongue along the woman's nose. Unprepared for a wet kiss, the woman reared back––grimacing and squealing.

Grace pressed her finger down and then looked at the resulting picture on the phone's screen. She chuckled before showing it to Clover.

Grinning from ear-to-ear, Clover weighed in. "Perfect."

The woman was holding Star out away from her now. Grace took advantage of her distraction, grabbing the squirming animal, and handing back the lady's phone. "Enjoy the rest of your day." She smiled at the woman before shuffling away with her two little girls in tow.

Once they were out of earshot, Clover added under her breath, "You're welcome for the free nose cleaning."

Grace couldn't help it. She tipped her head back and guffawed with laughter at her silly and witty daughter.

They smiled at each other over their unpredictable puppy. "There's never a dull moment with you two," Grace said to her child.

Clover grinned up at her, revealing the dark hole where her front tooth should be. "I think the fun is just beginning," she guessed.

Grace nodded in full agreement with her daughter's assessment and wondered what hilarity would be coming next with their crazy, now-famous puppy.

*a*s soon as they walked into Marlene's side of the house, the woman rushed forward to greet them. "We always knew you were special, but now the entire Gold Coast knows," she said directly to the puppy.

"Yeah, she's already getting recognized by her adoring fans." Grace rolled her eyes at her friend.

"Really?" Marlene seemed excited by that development. At Grace's nod, she went on. "You're destined for big things, Little Star."

Clover ran off to the playroom. Since Marlene's kids were at school, she could enjoy the special treat of having the entire area to herself.

By the time Grace situated herself on her usual stool at the counter, Marlene had placed a piping hot mug of tea in front of her. "I think she might really be," Grace agreed with her friend's assessment. "I just signed a contract with lots of zeroes on the dollar amount for her to continue on the show."

"What? That's fantastic!" Grace didn't detect a bit of jealousy in Marlene's voice.

She nodded to confirm before adding, "They offered her a one-year contract, with an option to renew. We'll see how it's going at that point, but at least for now, the audience loves her."

"Of course they do." Marlene looked over at the puppy, who was already snuggled up with Suzie Q and napping peacefully after her hard hour of work.

Sounding like a proud mom, Grace revealed, "They said it was the highest ratings the show has had since they scored the only interview "O" has done in the last few years."

"It's going to continue to get better as word spreads about Star joining the show. She was absolutely adorable, and she brings some much-needed comedic relief to the endless droning of Dash Diamond." Marlene sounded like she was as proud of Star as Grace was, but Grace was surprised to hear her bashing of the show's host.

Furrowing her brow, Grace commented, "I thought Dash Diamond was beloved by all."

"He's okay, I guess." Marlene shrugged her shoulders.

Grace couldn't explain her odd urge to defend the pompous host. Shoving that down, she said instead, "He's kind of a jerk in real life."

"I'm not a bit surprised to hear that," Marlene weighed in.

For some strange reason, her harsh judgment of Dash raised Grace's hackles. She was tempted to find a way to stick up for him, which made absolutely no sense. Not wanting to offend her friend, she remained quiet as she pondered her odd protective instinct for the egotistical morning show host.

Not sensing Grace's turmoil on the subject, Marlene went on. "Our sweet little Star will humanize him, though."

"I hope so," Grace answered honestly, even though she doubted that was in the realm of possibility, given Dash's strong dislike of the animal.

Suddenly feeling the urge to leave, Grace stood and yelled towards the playroom, "Clover, time to go."

Marlene looked somewhat taken aback by Grace's abrupt shift. "You haven't even finished your tea," she lightly chastised her.

Grace took one more sip. "Sorry, I have a lot of things to get done today."

Heading to the dog bed, she lifted the snoozing puppy, who barely opened her eyes at the commotion. Grace hoped Marlene wouldn't question her about what all of these 'things' were that she needed to accomplish. Normally, she shared every detail of her days with Marlene, but for some reason, she just wanted to be alone with her little family in her own home right now.

"Okay, see you in the morning." Marlene gave her a warm smile, indicating that she held no hard feelings about Grace's sudden departure.

Clover came to the kitchen and whined about leaving, since she rarely got to play at Marlene's without the other kids.

Grace shut her down with a quick and firm, "We're going home."

As Grace followed her moping daughter, she turned to close the door behind them. Marlene said just loud enough for Grace to hear, "Have fun daydreaming about Dash Diamond."

Grace's cheeks flared pink as she realized her friend had figured out what was going on even before she did. Somehow that arrogant, self-important, vain, and crabby-when-not-on-camera man had managed to get under her skin!

Grace and Clover quickly assimilated Star's new work schedule into their early-morning routine. As soon as she got up, Grace fed Star breakfast and let her outside in the fenced-in backyard. Once Grace was ready, she took Clover and Star to Marlene's house, where Clover liked to watch a morning cartoon and join the other kids for breakfast before school.

Marlene walked Star and all of the kids to their early-morning school bus stop, giving Star a bit of exercise. They usually returned home about five minutes before Star's limo arrived to deliver her to the studio.

Their routine worked like a well-oiled machine. Little seemed to have changed in their lives, except when Grace had a spare moment to glance at the bakery's tiny television screen during the 9 o'clock hour and see her puppy on live television. That part of it was completely surreal.

The grocery where she worked was a chain store, but their regular customers made it feel more like a mom-and-pop shop. Grace had placed a framed picture of Clover and Star on the counter, which patrons fawned over. It wasn't unusual for Grace to have a ten-minute, over-the-counter conversation with an older gentleman who reminisced about the Golden Retrievers he had growing up, or with a twenty-something woman who wanted to laugh with her about Star's latest antics on the show.

Grace marveled at how much people seemed to relate to and care about her little dog. Star was a great conversation starter, and it seemed she was almost universally beloved in the greater Gold Coast region. There was only one glaring exception to that rule––Dash Diamond.

The longer the show went on, the more obvious it became that the show's host could barely tolerate the presence of its four-legged mascot. As Star became more comfortable on the set, her natural inquisitiveness and tendency to poke her nose where it didn't belong became even more prevalent.

By their enthusiastic reactions, it was obvious that the show's audience and celebrity guests were charmed and delighted by the naughty puppy's antics. It wasn't unusual for her to "Woof!" at inopportune moments, walk over guests as they were trying to tell an engaging story, squeak her toys while Dash was mid-sentence, or chew on anything and everything that she shouldn't.

Grace was alarmed one morning when she didn't see Star on-camera during the opening monologue of the show. Normally, the puppy and Dash sat on the sofa as the host chatted and joked with viewers as if he were in their living rooms with them, while the puppy did everything in her power to get his attention. Dash was a pro at staunchly ignoring her, almost as if she didn't exist in his world. The audience was riveted by their bristly relationship.

For the first time in all the years Grace had been watching the show, Dash Diamond paused his wooing of viewers with his spellbinding banter, turned to someone off-camera, and asked, "Are we just going to let her electrocute herself?"

The camera view panned down to Star, who was sprawled on the floor, trying to chomp through one of the heavy-duty black cords running to the video equipment. Nora scurried out, scooped up the puppy, and plopped her down beside Dash before returning to her normal hiding spot.

Being a consummate professional, Dash would normally have carried on with the show as if nothing had gone awry. For some reason, though, he turned back to the camera with his close-up shot and deadpanned, "Don't think this means I like her... I just didn't want the studio to smell like fried dog for the next year."

The in-studio audience guffawed with laughter over his disgusting joke, but Grace froze in her twisting of a pretzel-shaped donut to stare at the screen. She had always assumed that somewhere, hidden very deep down inside him, Dash Diamond secretly liked Star. The schtick of him hating her worked for the show's dynamic, and the audience absolutely loved his stilted interactions with the puppy.

Was it possible that he truly hated her sweet pet?

*a*pparently, Grace wasn't the only one who noticed that Dash's supposed disdain for Star might truly be real. The show's producers called Grace in for a meeting later that day.

Convinced that Star was about to be fired, but grateful that her brush with fame had lasted as long as it had, Grace went to the studio as soon as her shift ended at the bakery.

Sitting around a big, shiny mahogany conference room table with Dash, Miles, Evelyn, and some studio bigwigs Grace didn't recognize, Grace listened to them ramble on about the latest control group opinions on Dash and Star's on-screen chemistry.

The man in the custom-tailored suit, who was sitting at the head of the massive table said, "The audience used to love it that Dash couldn't stand sharing the spotlight with Star, but now their opinions are starting to shift."

Grace assumed his next statement would be that they were booting Star off the show. She nodded, preparing herself to accept the news in a polite and professional manner.

She was shocked when he turned to face Dash and went on to say, "We think it's time for you to bond with and accept Star as your permanent co-host."

"Co-host?!?" Dash blustered as if this was the most ridiculous thing he had ever heard. "She's more of a mischievous show mascot... at best."

Grace bristled over his dismissal of her puppy, but before she could stick up for Star, the man at the head of the table boomed, "Star is staying, whether you like it or not."

Dash sat back in his chair. His mouth was slightly agape. He was obviously as stunned as Grace was about the potential implication of the studio executive's words. It had almost sounded like he was implying that Star would remain on the show and Dash would be replaced if they couldn't work this out.

When the weight of his words sank in around the table, the man softened his tone to say, "We would very much like for *both* of you to remain on the show, Dash."

Dash stared down at the table, remaining silent. It was obvious he was shocked by the revelation that Star was the one the studio would keep if it came down to a choice between the two of them.

Turning to the table at large, the man splayed his hands and continued, as if his words hadn't crushed Dash. "To that end, we would like for Dash and Star to spend some quality time together off-the-air. The two of them need to bond, so we think Star should move in with Dash for at least a week."

Heads nodded in agreement around the table––with two exceptions.

Grace had heard enough. Clover would be devastated to give up their puppy for an entire week. Besides, she didn't want Star to have to stay with a man who couldn't stand her. "I don't think that's a good idea," she said firmly at the same time as Dash said, "I don't want a dog in my condo." He wrinkled up his nose in distaste, as if the mere thought of Star being in his living space was revolting.

Unwilling to listen to their arguments, the man at the head of the table stood and said, "Figure out a way to make it work." Turning to Dash, he added, "You have seven days to prove you've bonded with that pup." He left no doubt about the finality of his words because he immediately stalked out of the room with the other suits hot on his heels.

Grace, Dash, Miles, and Evelyn were the only ones remaining at the large table. They gawked at each other, not quite able to believe what had just transpired.

Miles was the first to regain his composure. "This won't be so bad," he promised in his slick producer voice. His tone made him sound to Grace like he belonged on a cheesy used car commercial. At Dash's grumpy scowl, he added with a bit less confidence, "It's only a week."

"I would never get the dog hair or dog *smell* out of my condo," Dash groused.

Not wanting this to happen any more than Dash did, Grace jumped in. "I don't want Star having to live with someone who can barely tolerate her." Crossing her arms, she added, "It's not fair to rip her away from her loving and accepting family to go live with *him*." She nodded her head in Dash's direction.

It seemed like they were at a standstill when both she and Dash pointedly looked away from each other, with their arms crossed under their chests like stubborn and petulant children.

Grace practically heard the light bulb click on in Miles' head. Snapping his fingers, he said to Grace, "Dash can come stay at your place," as if he had discovered the perfect solution to all of their problems.

Dash and Grace both frowned at this proposal, but Evelyn was the first to speak. "Does she even have room for him?" Her crush on the morning show host was practically scrawled across her face.

Jumping on the other woman's argument, Grace said, "No, I don't have a spare bedroom. The best I would be able to offer is a lumpy sofa in my living room." She had been confident the arrogant host wouldn't stoop to living under her roof at all––especially not if he was relegated to sleeping on the couch.

Proving her right, Dash said sarcastically, "Hmm. Let me think about it... NO!" His refusal came out at the same moment as Miles was drawling, "Perfect."

Turning a confident and pragmatic smile in Dash's direction, Miles said, "It sounded to me like the alternative to bonding with Star was pretty clear." He let the unspoken threat of Dash's firing hang in the air.

The silence hung between the foursome for what seemed like an interminable length of time while Dash weighed his options. Evidently not coming up with another viable alternative, he finally said through gritted teeth, "Fine."

All eyes turned to Grace. She couldn't let Star go stay alone with a man who despised her, and she also couldn't stomach jeopardizing Dash's career. Feeling backed into a corner, she finally nodded her head in agreement as well.

With that gesture, it was settled. Wealthy, spoiled, and egotistical celebrity Dash Diamond was coming to live with Grace, Clover, and Star in their tiny two-bedroom row house apartment. What could possibly go wrong?

15

*O*nce the studio execs made their demand, things moved quickly to make it happen. Grace scrambled to clean her house before Dash's scheduled arrival. She always kept things tidy, but for some reason, she wanted everything spotless for his visit.

She told herself the cleaning frenzy was because her home was already smaller and less luxurious than what Dash was used to, so she didn't want him to notice dirt as well. Some deeply suppressed side of her knew that her sudden urge to manically clean was more than that, though.

Clover seemed amped up over the celebrity's arrival, too, as she raced around the house picking up her and Star's stray toys. They had never had anyone stay over in their home before--especially not a man--so this was a brand new experience for them.

Grace wasn't sure if Star picked up on their nervous energy or not. The puppy was super rambunctious-- pouncing at their feet as they walked by, acting more like a kitten than a puppy--but that wasn't overly unusual for the energetic animal.

When the time for Dash's arrival came and went with no sign of the man, Grace and Clover sat anxiously on the edge of their sofa. They were so tightly strung that the knock on the door startled them both.

Grace was surprised when she opened the door to find Marlene on the other side. They were daily visitors to her side of the house, but the woman rarely came to their apartment.

"Is he here?" Marlene stage-whispered.

Grace shook her head, glad Dash hadn't yet shown up because he most definitely would have heard Marlene's question about him.

Obviously hoping to be present for his appearance, Marlene came inside and sat down at their tiny kitchen table. As close as the women were, awkwardness prevailed from the role reversal of Marlene sitting in Grace's kitchen.

"Umm, would you like some coffee?" As soon as the words left her mouth, Grace realized it was too late for her early-rising friend to drink caffeine. She mentally inventoried the supplies in her kitchen. "Or chocolate milk?" she offered uncertainly.

Trying to alleviate Grace's obvious nervousness about hosting her for once, Marlene said, "I'm perfectly fine, dear. Sit down and relax for a minute." Marlene patted the table beside her to enunciate her words.

Before Grace made it over to the table to sit down, a loud rap echoed on the front door. Without waiting for a response, the visitor flung the door, which Grace had failed to re-lock after Marlene's arrival, wide open. Grace was too taken aback by the rude intrusion to be frightened.

Entering her home with a flourish, grandly waving his arms about, Dash announced in his booming stage voice, "Dash Diamond is here!"

The ladies––including the puppy––gawked at him,

blinking and trying to comprehend what had just happened. Grace turned to lock eyes with Marlene, and the two women struggled not to burst into giggles over the man's ridiculous entrance.

Clover furrowed her tiny brows together as she looked up at him. "Why do you talk about yourself like you're not you?" she asked him logically.

Obviously not used to being questioned about his obnoxious use of the third person when referring to himself, Dash dropped his arms and attempted to explain. "Well, I am Dash Diamond," he told her, as if that explained everything.

Not one to be easily brushed aside when she wanted to dig into something, Clover responded, "Well, I am Clover Wilson, but I don't yell it out when I walk into a room."

"But I'm a celebrity." Dash enunciated the word 'celebrity' like it should be accompanied by jazz hands.

Refusing to be shot down, Clover said, "So is Star, but we don't announce her arrival everywhere we go."

Dash inhaled a deep breath, obviously getting ready to make a rebuttal for Clover's argument, but Marlene shut him down by standing to leave. "I think I've seen enough," she said near Grace's ear as she gave her a reassuring hug. As she walked past Dash towards the door, she bellowed, "Marlene Barnes is leaving!"

Grace couldn't contain the burst of laughter that bubbled up, even though an odd cringing sensation occurred deep in her belly over Dash and Marlene's unfortunate introduction.

She knew her friend had already been convinced that the celebrity was a self-important, arrogant jerk. Dash's over-the-top arrival had done nothing to soften that opinion. In fact, Marlene was probably now certain that Dash was full-of-himself, and she was right. Grace couldn't put her finger on why that bothered her so much.

Once they were alone, the awkward silence ensued.

Wanting to ensure he was aware that his peacock-like posturing didn't impress her, Grace suggested firmly, "While you're living with us, maybe you should refrain from the obnoxious third-person introductions of yourself when you enter the room."

Dash's head whipped back slightly as if she had slapped him. Grace guessed she was the first person to ever chastise the powerful celebrity. He was probably used to people bending over backwards to do his bidding. Grace wanted to make sure it was clear from the start that he wouldn't be coddled here. She had enough responsibilities without mothering him too.

Seeming to look at her with new eyes, even though they were the same startling blue they had always been, Dash said, "I'll try to refrain." The grin he gave her was almost self-effacing.

Just as Grace was wondering if her rational, firm approach had gotten through to the spoiled star already, he shifted gears yet again. "Where is Dash Diamond's room? He needs his beauty rest because he gets up early."

Grace shook her head at the exasperating, obnoxious man. Unable to resist, she pointed at her couch. "Dash Diamond is visiting Sofa City tonight," she informed him glibly before putting her arm around Clover, scooping up the puppy, and leaving the spoiled celebrity to stare after her in stunned silence.

16

*G*race was too fired up to sleep. Instead, she paced her room like a nervous cat. "Who does HE think he is?" she hissed quietly, before turning to walk to the other side of the room. "He thinks he can come into MY house and act all hoity-toity?" She turned again. "How dare he act like he's better than us?" After turning once more, she realized, "He didn't even interact with Star. Isn't that the point of all of this?!?"

Deciding she was going to wear a track in the already threadbare carpet, Grace plopped down on the edge of her bed and ran a hand anxiously through her long hair.

Despite his poor manners and unprecedented level of conceit, she wanted Dash to be comfortable in her home. She had set a pillow, as well as folded sheets and blankets, on the sofa for him. He was a tall man—easily over six feet—so she imagined that he was hanging off both ends of her couch.

She was tempted to go out and offer to swap places with him. She could easily fit on the couch, so it would be a more comfortable night's sleep for her out there than him. Forcing herself to remember his entitled behavior, she refrained from offering to switch sleeping arrangements with him.

When she went to the drawer containing her pajamas, she pulled out the cute matching cotton set Marlene had given her for Christmas last year, rather than any of the assorted shorts and ratty tee shirts she normally slept in. She refused to wonder about why she cared how she looked on this particular night.

It was a restless night for Grace as she tossed and turned and tried not to worry about how uncomfortable Dash might be. It simply wasn't in her nature to be inhospitable––no matter how undeserving her houseguest might be.

When her 4:30 a.m. alarm went off, she awoke feeling groggy. She was usually a great sleeper. She normally felt refreshed and ready to face her day when she awoke, but last night she hadn't slept well at all. Now, she understood why so many people liked sleeping in late. She would have given anything to roll over and doze off, but she didn't have that option.

When she stumbled out of her room, she was infuriated to find the bathroom was already occupied. She knew Clover would still be sleeping soundly, so it was obvious who was in there hogging all the hot water.

Trying not to let the interruption to her finely-tuned routine bother her, Grace decided to make breakfast. She normally only did that on weekends because through the week, Clover ate at Marlene's and Grace just grabbed an apple or banana to eat on her way to the bakery.

Since they had a guest, who was knocking her schedule out of whack anyway, Grace made waffles. She hummed to herself as she whisked the batter, refusing to let irritation over the bathroom situation ruin her morning. After all, if she skipped sipping her morning mug of English Breakfast tea, while rocking in her chair and perusing Facebook on her phone, she would be right back on schedule.

To her delight, she heard Dash singing the old-school upbeat song *Footloose* in the shower. It was so rare to find another happy morning person. Most people she encountered––including her sweet Clover and the otherwise marvelous Marlene––were grumpy Gus's in the early morning hours. In fact, Grace's chipper morning attitude was known to irritate both Clover and Marlene to no end.

Dash's singing wasn't exactly what anyone would call 'good,' but it was charming, nonetheless. It was refreshing to encounter a fun and carefree side of him that wasn't in any way conceited or entitled.

Grace made the waffles one-at-a-time in their Mickey Mouse-shaped iron. She also washed and sliced fresh strawberries, heated maple syrup, and put a pan of bacon in the oven. Once she had the table set with the good plates that she normally reserved for holidays and other special occasions, she filled three of her four crystal champagne flutes with orange juice. She wasn't sure why she was trying so hard to impress the insufferable man in her bathroom, but she didn't seem to be able to stop herself.

Once she had the waffles made and the bacon pulled out of the oven, Grace plopped down on one of her mismatched kitchen chairs to sip her steaming mug of tea. She couldn't believe the shower was still running. How long was he going to stay in there?? They had never actually run out of hot water on her side of the house, but they just might today. The last thing she wanted was a lukewarm or chilly shower.

Deciding she didn't want to let the food get cold while waiting for 'His Highness' to finally emerge from the bathroom, she went to wake up Clover. The little girl grumbled, but shuffled after her mother out to the kitchen.

With impeccable timing, Dash emerged from the bathroom. A damp cloud of steam wafted out into the hallway in his wake. "Something smells fabulous!"

At least he was enthusiastic about the meal. Grace didn't want him to expect the star-treatment from her every morning, so she told him, "Don't get used to it."

Checking out the setup, Dash turned towards Grace as if truly seeing her for the first time. "How could I not get used to all of this?"

His semi-flirty statement was the first kind thing he had said since his arrival at Grace, Clover, and Star's small home. Grace silently cursed the heat that flared visibly on her cheeks.

Dash quickly ruined the moment by asking, "Is this meal gluten-free, vegan, and organic?" When she simply bugged her eyes out at him, he added, "And do you have any chilled bottles of blueberry-coconut fusion water?"

When she simply stared at him, not quite able to believe his audacity, he added, "Don't worry about it. I'll make my usual stop by Cup of Joe Diner on my way in to work. They know what I like. Oh, and I need a towel warmer in the bathroom. How can you stand there freezing while you dry off with those unheated towels?"

Shaking her head and rolling her eyes in Clover's direction, Grace said under her breath, "I think it's going to be a long week."

*D*ash picked at a few strawberries and sipped the cup of black coffee Grace had slammed in front of him—practically daring him to complain. Grace went to the back door to keep an eye on Star as she searched the fenced-in backyard for the perfect spot to do her business.

Once he finished his incredibly light breakfast, Dash walked over to grab his leather attaché case. "See you tonight, dear," he joked, his vivid blue eyes sparkling in Grace's direction.

Joining in on the silly banter, Grace teased him right back. "Can't wait, hon."

For her part, drowsy Clover bugged her eyes out at both of them like they had lost their minds. She had never before seen her mother interact with a handsome man—especially not in their home—so this was an all-new experience to her.

With that, Dash slipped past Grace and was out the door. All of a sudden, it dawned on her that the insufferable man still hadn't so much as spoken to Star—let alone bonded with her.

"Don't you want to take Star with you?" she yelled after him, but he was already out of earshot––or at least pretending he was.

Once she called Star inside, Grace sat down with her little girl to eat their special weekday waffle and bacon breakfast. They didn't enjoy their usual easy banter because Clover looked like she would have preferred resting her head on the table and dozing back off, rather than eating. The little girl managed to stay awake, but she didn't look happy about it.

As they ate, Grace glanced into the living room and was surprised to see Dash's sheets and blankets folded and stacked into a neat pile on the sofa. She grudgingly admitted the gesture was a little bit endearing.

In no way did that one thoughtful and kind deed counteract his numerous annoying features, she reminded herself as she padded to the bathroom to take her hopefully-not-frigid shower. As she closed the door behind her, she smiled, closed her eyes, and deeply inhaled the damp, fragrant air. The scent was outdoorsy with a hint of some mysterious masculine aroma that made her heart feel like it might thump out of her chest.

Once she moved beyond the delightful man-smell, she quickly realized Dash's primping products had overtaken her bathroom. His hair gel, shaving supplies, and deodorant were sprawled across every inch of flat space on her spotless white porcelain pedestal sink. The shower had been invaded to an even greater degree. Dash had certainly left his mark––by way of expensive hair-loss prevention treatment bottles, a fancy glass bottle of shower gel, and an enormous loofah back scratcher that was hanging to dry in front of her mesh cleansing sponge.

It seemed foreign and oddly intimate to be sharing shower space with the pampered celebrity. Thinking about it made Grace's tummy do a little flip-flop--until she realized there was not, in fact, any hot water left.

As she shivered in the quickest shower she had ever taken, Grace decided she would need to have a firm talk with Dash about limiting the length of his showers. That, or she could just make sure to get up and in here before him, so he would see first-hand what it was like when his extended grooming routine emptied the water heater tank.

Envisioning the almighty Dash Diamond huddled and freezing in a cold shower made Grace chuckle. There was something larger-than-life about the celebrity that made her mental image particularly gratifying. She refused to allow her mind to wonder how the irritating man had managed to weasel his way under her skin so thoroughly.

Not surprisingly, the interaction on the show between Dash and Star didn't improve that morning. If anything, he managed to ignore her more than normal. It almost seemed like he thought if he didn't acknowledge her, she would cease to exist in his world.

For her part, Star seemed to take his intentional disregard as a challenge to get him to acknowledge her in some way-- even if it meant she had to annoy him until he was furious.

Grace couldn't help but chuckle as she watched Star attack Dash's expensive Italian leather shoes--while he was wearing them--in a vain attempt to get his attention during his opening monologue.

Without missing a beat in his one-way conversation with viewers, Dash picked up a throw pillow from the sofa where he was seated and placed it on the floor to block the puppy from his feet.

Not to be deterred, Star made her way around to the other side of the table to chomp on Dash's left shoe.

Smoothly placing the sofa's other brightly-hued pillow between his shoe and the puppy, Dash flashed his winning smile and continued.

Proving she was as stubborn as she was cute, Star moved to the front of the table that sat in front of the sofa. The camera panned out so viewers could see what she was doing. Evidently deciding this was the best way to get to Dash's irresistible shoes, the puppy squatted down and moved forward, like a soldier creeping under a low-lying mattress of barbed wire in an obstacle course.

The in-studio audience practically tittered as they watched the strong-willed puppy slowly make her way towards her forbidden prize. When she finally made it and clamped down on Dash's shoe, the crowd cheered like she had just made a game-winning touchdown.

For the first time, Dash acknowledged the ornery puppy's antics. Turning to someone off-screen, he said through gritted teeth, "I seem to be out of pillows to block this little…"

When he paused to search for a word to call Star, Grace was certain his barely-contained fury was tempting him to call the puppy a brat or demon-dog.

Despite his fuming anger, he retained his wits enough to know the crowd would turn on him for insulting Star. He finally landed on the innocuous word "pup" to complete his dangling sentence.

Evidently sensing that the host was at his wit's end, an off-screen decision was made and Nora rushed forward to whisk the animal away.

Breathing a visible sigh of relief at Star's departure and quickly placing the pillows back on the couch, Dash resumed the show with a new level of enthusiasm.

Despite the host's newfound passion, the remainder of the show––after Star's departure––felt flat to Grace. When she got the call from the show's producers requesting an urgent meeting that afternoon, she knew she wasn't the only one who had noticed.

*S*lamming his fist down on the shiny mahogany conference table, Dash yelled, "This is ridiculous!"

Obviously wanting to seem sympathetic to the host's dismay, Miles said calmly, "Ridiculous or not, the viewers have spoken. They want Star." He let that sink in for a moment before revealing, "We've never had as many outraged calls and emails as we did today after you had her forcibly removed from the set."

Grace thought the 'forcibly' wording was a little strong, but decided it was in her best interest to remain quiet until Dash had a minute to calm down. He was obviously reeling from the very thinly-veiled threat issued by the studio executives.

What it boiled down to was that Dash was to spend every waking moment of the next week with Star. If they determined that the two hadn't properly bonded by the end of that timeframe, then they would find a replacement for the host of the show... one who actually liked dogs.

"Look, Dash, we're all rooting for you," the suit at the head of the table said kindly. Proving he was a cutthroat businessperson at heart, he went on, "But the numbers don't lie. If you can't make this work with Star as your co-host, then we'll find someone who can."

As much as Dash's supreme confidence sometimes irritated Grace, she still hated seeing his shoulders slumped forward and the drawn, crestfallen look on his face. She had never seen the arrogant man look so dejected, and it was more than a little jarring.

Grace had expected the executives to make a quick exit, like they did last time, so when they lingered, she wondered what else they had on their agenda. She silently hoped it wasn't anything that would add to the downcast expression on Dash's face. He had endured enough today.

Pushing a button on the tablet beside him, the head honcho barked into the speaker, "Have Star brought in here."

As if she had been waiting directly outside the door, Nora entered with Star trotting proudly at her side. Grace noticed the studio had replaced the pup's purple nylon leash with a jewel-encrusted version to match her gaudy pendant and collar.

They obviously didn't want the puppy to fly under the radar when she was out in public. She was publicity gold, and they wanted her to be recognized and admired everywhere she went, unlike the currently downtrodden host of the show.

Grace hoped for Dash's sake that he could drum up a positive reaction to Star's appearance in the conference room. She could tell he tried, but the best he could summon was a half-hearted smile that didn't come close to reaching his eyes.

"Here's your constant companion for the week!" The executive's enthusiasm level sounded the same as if he had been announcing the winner of millions of dollars in the lottery.

"Hey, Star," Dash said flatly as he bent down to ruffle a hand over the puppy's ears.

It was the first time Grace had seen the celebrity directly acknowledge the little dog. If Star was surprised by the sudden shift in Dash's reaction to her, she didn't show it. She pushed her head up into his hand, demanding more attention——just like she did to everyone.

"Great!" the executive weighed in before standing, as if the matter was settled. "We'll look forward to seeing your progress with her," he added, giving Dash an ominous look before leading the parade of tailored dark gray suits out the door.

Silence reigned for a long moment in the conference room after the executives left. Dash stared wide-eyed at the floor, while the others looked around at each other, trying to figure out what they could say to comfort the obviously distraught man.

Seeming to come out of a trance, Dash scrubbed a hand over his face. "I think I'm going to go for a walk. I could use some fresh air," he said to no one in particular.

"That's a great idea!" Nora weighed in. Smoothly putting the leash in his hand, she added purposefully, "Star loves walks."

Grace had little doubt that Dash had intended to take his walk alone to try to process what had just transpired. Nora's firm hint that he needed to take Star with him made his face fall even more.

Grace feared the upset television host might break down in tears, and she did not want to embarrass him further by witnessing it. Looking down to dig in her purse, she pulled out the roll of blue plastic bags she always kept on hand and tore one off for him. "Here you go." She tried to sound upbeat and friendly as she handed it to him.

Dash looked perplexed as he accepted the baggy from her. "What's this for?"

Grace could feel her cheeks burning hot. She didn't want to have to explain this to him, but Nora, Miles, and Evelyn remained silent behind her. Dash was blinking in her direction. He was obviously confused about why she thought he needed a bag.

Clearing her throat, she said, "That's in case Star has to… you know…" Bringing her voice down to a whisper, as if she were saying something truly scandalous, she finished, "Go number two."

Dash cringed back, but he still looked confused. "What does the bag have to do with anything?"

Grace knew she shouldn't have been surprised that he was so obtuse about these things. Answering his question, she said, "Well, you can't just leave it there for someone to step in." She let the implication hang between them, but Dash's brow was still furrowed in confusion.

Taking the bag back from him, and sticking her hand in to mimic the motion, she said, "You'll need to pick it up."

The color drained from Dash's face. "I think I'm going to be sick." Putting one hand over his mouth and using the other to snatch the offending bag back from Grace, he ran ashen-faced from the room.

Star trotted happily behind him on her leash as if they were heading on the best adventure of her life.

Grace forced down her churning nerves and silently prayed that her sweet puppy wasn't embarking on a disastrous week of epic proportions.

19

*G*race was surprised, when she arrived home after stopping back by the grocery to pick up a few things, to see Dash and Star sitting on her back porch steps. Marlene must have been out trying to get her errands done before picking up the kids from the school bus stop. As much as Grace knew her friend wanted to disapprove of Dash, Marlene's innate hospitality wouldn't have allowed her to leave him sitting outside on the stoop—especially not with Star in tow.

She sent a quick text to Marlene indicating that Clover could come straight home before sitting down beside Dash and Star. She placed her two reusable canvas bags on the steps, and inserted extra friendliness in her voice when she said, "Hi, I would have thought you two would go out and about for a while before coming home." She inwardly cringed a little at her implication that this was Dash's home. She wouldn't have been surprised if he wrinkled his nose in distaste at that thought.

"I'm not sure how to take care of her," Dash admitted, somewhat sheepishly.

It dawned on Grace then that he might be intending to try to get her to care for the puppy this week, while he sat idly by. When he reached out his hand to touch hers, she attempted––rather unsuccessfully––to ignore the zinging electricity she experienced from his touch and to stay focused on her irritation that he thought he could use her.

Jerking her hand back, and immediately missing the warmth of his touch, she said, "So, you thought you could come here and I would cover for you?" Taking a deep breath and trying to calm her voice, she added, "Even if I wanted to, I couldn't do that. People will be able to tell if your connection with Star after this week of forced bonding is genuine or pretend."

"I know," Dash admitted, sounding rather forlorn, before quickly adding, "And that really wasn't my intent." Looking down and kicking his foot at the ground, he admitted, "I like spending time here."

Grace was flabbergasted by his admission. She had assumed he was forcing himself to endure her household. Wondering about his sincerity, she turned to face him. "It has to be a big step down from your home."

His bright blue gaze was beaming directly at her, making her breath come faster. He ruined the moment by responding. "Oh, it's a lot smaller than what I'm used to, and I'm having my maintenance guy come over later to install a towel warmer in your bathroom." Turning to gaze out at the yard, he softened his previous statement by adding, "But it's more of a true home than my sterile condo could ever be. I might live in the penthouse of my building, but you have created a happy, safe, and loving respite for your little family that feels more like a real home than my bachelor pad ever will."

His assessment warmed her heart. She had always done her best to give Clover the kind of home she had dreamed of having when she was a little girl, but it felt marvelous to have his external validation——especially since Grace had assumed he didn't approve of anything about her or the life she had built for herself. "I try my best." She smiled at him.

"I can see that," he told her, sounding sincere. "Miss Clover is a lucky little lady to have you for a mom."

Embarrassed by his praise, Grace looked down and thanked him before indicating the grocery bags. I had better get these inside before the ice cream melts.

"Did someone say ice cream?" Dash sounded enthusiastic as he took the bags and followed her inside. Star bounded behind them.

"It's not gluten-free, fat-free, or dairy-free," she warned him, only partially teasing, before adding, "It's just plain old Breyer's mint chocolate chip.

"That sounds delicious!" he practically gushed as he set the bags on the counter. "Do you know how long it has been since I've had regular ice cream that hasn't been stripped of calories, fat, and flavor?"

Grace shook her head, silently wondering why he denied himself of so much.

"It's been a really long time," he answered vaguely. "Maybe we can have some after dinner?"

His eyes were so filled with hope, there was no way Grace could have denied him the treat. "Of course," she smiled and nodded. Dash's face lit up like a small child's at the prospect of ice cream for dessert.

As Grace put the groceries away in her tiny kitchenette, Dash attempted to help. She noticed he put everything in the wrong place, but she didn't correct him. Deciding it was the thought that counted, she tried to keep a mental inventory of everything that needed to be relocated sometime when Dash wasn't around.

Since they were sharing such a small space, Grace sensed

the moment the new idea registered in his mind. It didn't take long for him to voice it. "Can we order a big, greasy, extra cheese and pepperoni pizza for dinner?" he asked excitedly, before justifying the request. "I've had a really rough couple of days."

Grace couldn't help but chuckle at his enthusiasm, even as she wondered why he felt the need to defend a simple pizza craving. He was looking at her with that hope-filled gaze again, like a little kid, as he waited for her response. Putting him out of the misery of waiting, she said, "Sure, that sounds great."

Larger than life Dash Diamond whooped with excitement over her agreement to order pizza for dinner. She shook her head at the silly man. He truly was an enigma.

Clover burst through the front door at that moment and ran over to greet her excited puppy. She lifted Star and twirled her around, but nearly stumbled when she saw Dash in their kitchen. "Oh... hi." She sounded like she had forgotten Dash would be spending the week with them.

"Hi, sweetheart," Grace greeted her little girl before asking, "Did you have a good day?"

"Yeah," she responded noncommittally.

Unable to contain his excitement, Dash said to Clover, "We're having pizza for dinner and ice cream for dessert!"

"Yay!" Clover smiled so wide that her freckled little nose wrinkled. Grace couldn't get over how adorable the little girl looked. "Pizza is something with cheese, please!" her daughter enthused, revealing their mother-daughter inside joke about their penchant for gooey, melted cheese on their meals. Whenever they couldn't decide what to eat, Clover would exclaim that she wanted something with 'cheese, please!'

Putting the last of the groceries away and marveling that something so small as ordering pizza and digging into a container of ice cream could make the two of them so happy, Grace decided to make another suggestion. "I was thinking we could all walk down to the park."

"Yes!" Clover quickly agreed, as Grace had known she would.

"That sounds nice," Dash weighed in, before adding with a smile, "We'll earn those calories for tonight."

Once they had all taken turns in the bathroom and changed into comfy clothes and shoes, they reconvened in the living room. Grace bent to attach Star's sparkly leash to her collar before pointedly handing it to Dash.

Proving he was still Dash Diamond, the man leaned in and asked, "You'll take care of the baggy if we need one, right?"

Grace couldn't help it--she tipped her head back and laughed. Once she had her laughter under control, she looked up at Dash to say, "I think it's time you learned." With that, she sauntered out of the house, but not before she glimpsed the look of pure terror that washed over Dash's features.

When Clover caught up to her on the sidewalk, Grace put her arm around her daughter's tiny shoulders. "One thing is for sure," she informed her, "This week with Dash is bound to be anything but dull."

She couldn't have predicted how much truth was infused into that particular statement.

20

*T*he trio sat on the living room floor and ate pizza from paper plates around Grace's coffee table. They were in the midst of a raucous game of *Sorry!*

If Grace hadn't known better, she would have sworn by the carefree expression on Dash's face that the man was actually having fun with them. Surely, this simple night in couldn't compare with his usual wealthy celebrity bachelor lifestyle.

Star was sound asleep and curled up by Dash's side-- evidently thrilled to not have him trying to shove her away on live television.

Dash didn't sound a bit sorry as he said the word and knocked one of Grace's yellow game pieces, which had been nearing 'Home' back to the 'Start' position.

Grace pretended to be furious as she looked to the ceiling and said, "NO!" Her over-the-top reaction had Clover giggling with glee.

Evidently feeling confident, now that he had sent one of Grace's pieces back to the beginning, Dash said, "We should make this game a little more interesting by adding some stakes."

"What's that?" Clover asked.

Just as Grace was getting ready to explain that she didn't think gambling on a game with her young child was a good idea, Dash answered simply, "Stakes make it better to win." Before Grace could voice her concern with his line of thought, Dash added, "How about if the loser has to scoop the ice cream?"

Clover's eyes lit up. "Yes, that's a good stakes."

Her slight misuse of the word had the adults locking eyes over her head and smiling. Grace was relieved to hear that Dash wasn't intending to bet money on the game with her daughter.

"That sounds fair," Grace agreed to the challenge, even though it was beginning to look like she was going to lose. It wasn't much of a concession, since she had assumed she would be the one dipping the ice cream for everyone anyway.

Clover easily won the board game as she almost always did. But in a surprise twist, Grace came up from behind with a few drawn out "Sorrrry's" and beat Dash.

"You didn't sound at all sorry on that last one," Dash told her, accepting the loss good-naturedly.

"I wasn't," Grace answered honestly, grinning at him.

"You have to dip the ice cream!" Clover pointed her finger at Dash.

Grace was preparing to let him off the hook when he said, "You're right... Now, where do you keep the ice cream? In the oven?" He pretended to be completely dense.

Clover giggled with delight at his antics. "No, silly, in the fweezer," she informed him. Grace secretly liked it when Clover's slight mispronunciations occasionally popped out. As she got older, they were becoming fewer and farther between. They tended to only surface now when she so excited that she forgot to carefully watch her words.

"The freezer?" Dash asked, furrowing his brow like he was completely perplexed. "Is that this thing?" He pointed to the microwave.

Clover cackled at the silly man. "No, over there." She pointed to the fridge.

"Oh, this." He sounded confident as he opened the refrigerator door and searched for the ice cream.

"No, on the other side." Clover giggled, obviously thoroughly enjoying his game.

By the time he tried to get plates and forks for their ice cream and attempted to scoop out the frozen dessert with a spatula, Clover went to his side to supervise.

Grace moved up to the couch to watch and listen to them. She had to admit it was nice to have a male presence in their lives. Dash brought a laid-back and silly element to their lives––when he wasn't busy acting like a hoity-toity celebrity tool.

She was touched when he yelled into the living room, "Don't you have any vanilla ice cream for Star?"

Grace shook her head, suddenly feeling bad for not thinking of it before.

Bringing Grace's bowl and his, Dash asked, "Dogs can't have chocolate, right?"

"Yes, that's right," Grace answered, accepting the bowl from him.

He sat right beside her, and Clover plopped down on his other side with her bowl of mint chip. Star moved in and squeezed her way between Dash and Clover's feet.

It suddenly dawned on Grace that all three of them were surrounding Dash. Even in her own home, he had somehow managed to become the celebrity.

When he leaned down to pat Star on the head, he said,

"I'm sorry you don't get any ice cream. We'll get you some vanilla for the rest of the week."

Grace was impossibly touched that Dash seemed to be having his first true moment of bonding with Star. She'd had her doubts, but perhaps this week of togetherness would work after all.

She was smiling and thinking of what a perfect, happy picture the four of them must be when Dash added, "I'll get you some vanilla myself, since your mean, old mom didn't bother."

It took Grace a second to process what he had said. "Mean, old mom?!?" she practically spluttered.

The shake of his shoulders as he laughed made it obvious he had been teasing and was enjoying her reaction immensely.

Not one to be outdone, Grace spooned some of her ice cream and swiped it across Dash's nose.

Grace wondered if she had gone too far when Dash sat motionless, staring at her in stunned silence. She guessed no one had ever done such an outlandish thing to the pampered celebrity, and he obviously wasn't at all sure how to react.

Setting his bowl down on the table, Dash turned to fully face her. "That's it!" he practically yelled. Leaning in close to her face, he said, "Lick it off."

"Eww, no!" she squealed, tilting her head back.

"Will you lick it off?" he leaned towards Clover.

"Yuck, no way!" The little girl reared back.

Standing to retrieve a paper towel from the kitchen, Dash said over his shoulder. "Star would probably be thrilled to clean it off for me, but she can't have chocolate."

Once he had his face cleaned off, Dash returned to his spot on the couch, picked up his bowl, and began eating as if nothing were amiss.

Grace felt shocked he was going to let it go that easily, so she wasn't too surprised when he said under his breath, "I'll bide my time, but I will get even."

Her heart fluttered in her chest at the thought. As much as she hated to admit it, Grace was drawn to this new, fun side of Dash Diamond. She couldn't wait to see how he would retaliate.

21

*T*hey had too fun of an evening for Grace to reprimand Dash about his extra-long showers. She decided she would bring it up in the morning, if it happened again.

After they said their goodnights, she tucked in Clover and went to her own room. Once inside, she worried over what jammies she should wear. Her options were to re-wear the cute matching set she wore last night or to put on one of her old concert tee-shirts and a pair of shorts that had seen better days.

She wasn't even sure if she would bump into Dash before she was dressed in the morning, and it was a little disconcerting to be so concerned about what she wore to bed. She normally grabbed whatever was on top––whether it matched or not. She refused to think about why she was taking so much care with it now.

Frustrated and wanting to prove to herself that she truly didn't care what the normally-exasperating, occasionally-charming man in her living room thought, she grabbed her black Muse tee with the stretched-out collar and a pair of lime green shorts from her drawer. If that ensemble didn't say that she wasn't concerned with what Dash Diamond thought of her, nothing would.

Once she had changed and climbed into bed, she cursed herself, even as she tried to figure out a way for him not to see her in this old, mismatched ensemble. *So much for not caring what he thinks*, she silently chastised herself.

After a restless night of tossing, turning, thinking, and doing everything except sleeping, Grace hopped out of bed before her alarm went off. Today was a new day, and she refused to allow Dash Diamond to ruin her shower again.

Grabbing her work uniform and undergarments, she opened her bedroom door and bolted for the bathroom. It was still dark, so she let out a loud "Oomph!" of surprise when she ran directly into Dash in the hallway.

He reached around to flick the switch for the bathroom light. The intense light nearly blinded them both with its sudden brightness. Grace blinked, startled and trying to recalibrate. Dash recuperated faster and pointed down at the clothes Grace had dropped––intimate items up, of course.

"Pretty." Dash pointed to the pale pink wisps of fabric on the floor. He waggled his dark, perfectly-groomed eyebrows suggestively at her, which made her feel even more flustered.

Her cheeks burning hot with an odd mixture of embarrassment and intrigue, Grace bent and quickly scooped up her clothing. "Sorry, you weren't meant to see that," she explained as she tried to scoot by him in the hallway. She wanted to escape to the bathroom so she could regroup, calm down, and ponder if he was actually flirting with her or if his implied interest had simply been a typical male reaction.

"Don't ever apologize for that. Now it's the only thing I will be able to think about all day." He winked at her, leaving absolutely no doubt that he was, in fact, flirting with her.

Grace was so flustered by the entire interaction that she

failed to stop Dash as he slid into the bathroom and closed the door behind him.

Stomping back into her bedroom, she wanted to scream in frustration. How could that man be so charming and delightful one moment, but then turn right around and be an infuriating, self-centered pig?!? "It's MY bathroom," she fumed to her empty bedroom as she paced. "He should have to work around my schedule… not the other way around."

Talking to herself got her sufficiently fired up to confront him. Barging back out into the hallway, she lifted her fist to pound on the bathroom door and insist he let her shower first.

She paused with her fist held in mid-air. Instead of cheery singing, Dash was whistling happily today. She quickly recognized the tune as "Zip-a-dee-doo-dah."

Grace's lips turned up, despite her justified annoyance. It was difficult to remain angry with someone who whistled about what a wonderful day it was so early in the morning.

She rarely encountered other natural morning people. Even her early-morning customers at the bakery were usually either in search of a quick sugar-high to help them endure their first few hours at work or looking for a small bribe for their co-workers or boss.

Her overtired first customers of the day usually mumbled a "thank you" to her and shuffled to the checkout lanes, without ever actually making eye contact with her.

Dash's chipper whistling distracted her enough from her anger that she knocked just loudly enough to get his attention before hissing at him through the door, trying not to wake Clover. "You better leave me some hot water––unlike yesterday." Her toned-down threat didn't sound nearly as harsh as she had intended when she stormed out of her bedroom to give him a piece of her mind.

"Sure thing," he responded amiably back at her.

When silence ensued, it became obvious that no apology or chivalrous offer to let her shower first was forthcoming. Since she had lost much of the steam to her anger, she padded into the kitchen to wait for her turn in the shower.

Even though she knew Dash was supposed to be caring for Star, she couldn't justify making the puppy wait to go outside or eat her breakfast. Besides, who knew how long it would be before the blasted man was ready?

Once Star was digging into her puppy chow, Grace carefully folded her undies inside her work uniform to ensure she wouldn't flash her delicates at Dash again. Even though she hadn't been wearing them at the time, it seemed way too intimate for the celebrity to know what her skivvies looked like. She couldn't help wondering if he would really give it more thought today. *Would he think about her undergarments during his live TV show?* The mere thought of it made Grace's cheeks heat.

Shaking her head to clear that line of thought, she went to start her ancient coffee pot. While it spluttered to life, she used the microwave to heat up one of the day-old donuts she had brought home from the bakery yesterday. When the microwave's timer ticked down to a second, she quickly opened the door, not wanting the buzzing to wake up Clover before the little girl absolutely *had* to get up. She was well aware how much her daughter enjoyed and needed sleep, so Grace did her best to allow her as much as possible.

Enjoying the relative quiet, Grace ate her breakfast, drank her first cup of coffee, and perused the surprising number of emails she had received overnight. After she had finished everything she could outside of the bathroom and she still heard the shower running, she became irritated.

It was bad enough that Dash used all of the hot water yesterday, but today she had warned him about it, and he appeared to be doing the same thing––even though he knew it might leave her with a cold shower. His gall was infuriating!

Right as she was getting worked up enough to go bang on the door and demand he get out of the shower, she heard the water shut off. If he had tried to shorten his morning routine at all, it had only been by a minute or two. When he emerged, she intended to give him a strong talking to about the rules of sharing a bathroom.

She tapped her fingers in annoyance on the table as she waited for him to complete his--apparently extensive-- grooming routine. When he finally opened the door, she steeled herself to give him a firm talking to. As much as she hated conflict, she simply couldn't put up with an entire week of him hogging her bathroom.

When Dash walked into the kitchen, Star ran over to greet him. Her tail was wagging back and forth so hard it almost looked like she was bending herself in half on one side, then the other, in quick succession. When he bent down and said to the puppy, "Good morning, little one," Grace was charmed, despite her anger over the shower situation.

His apparent shift in attitude towards her dog worked to immediately diffuse her annoyance. She could feel her lips turning up as she watched the perfectly-coiffed man stooping to scratch the thrilled puppy.

When Star whirled around to bring Dash her favorite bouncy red ball, he complied by tossing it to the living room for her to retrieve. When he stood back up, he stared at his now-wet hand. "Yuck," he commented as he moved past Grace to get to the kitchen sink to wash his hands.

With his back to her as he scrubbed his hands at the sink, Dash said, "Muse, huh?"

It took Grace a moment to figure out that he was referring to her shirt. "Oh, yes," she said, staring down at the tattered shirt. "I can't seem to get enough of them," she admitted.

Turning as he dried his hands with her best kitchen towel, Dash said, "I like them, too. Maybe I should request that we get them booked for an appearance on the show. You should come to the studio to meet them when we get them scheduled."

She noticed he said 'when,' not 'if.' It was easy for Grace to forget he was *THE* Dash Diamond when he was using all of her hot water. His gentle reminder of his celebrity status had her gazing at him like a teenager with a crush on her science teacher.

Snapping herself out of her semi-daze, she purposefully kept her tone even as she said, "That sounds fun." She hoped she sounded nonchalant, even though her insides were doing a happy-dance at the thought of meeting one of her favorite bands of all time.

Grace tried to figure out a way to shift the conversation back to their bathroom schedule, but Dash surprised her by changing gears himself. "I was thinking that I could cook dinner tonight." His kind offer caught her completely off-guard.

"Oh." Her hand involuntarily lifted to her chest as she processed his words and tried to remind herself that he was here out of necessity, not in a dating capacity. "I didn't realize you could cook," she hedged.

"Yep," he answered proudly before adding, "Well, one meal... I make killer spaghetti. It's my great-grandmother's red sauce recipe."

"Wow, I can't wait," Grace responded sincerely, trying to nudge down her overwhelming surprise at his kind and generous offer. "Do you want to give me a list of ingredients, so I can pick them up before leaving the store?"

"Nope, I'll take care of everything." He grabbed one of the day-old donuts from the box on the counter.

Guilt suddenly overwhelmed her for serving him stale pastries, when he was planning to make her a homemade meal for dinner. Her plan had been to let him know that he shouldn't expect her to make waffles every morning, but now she was beginning to doubt her decision to be less than hospitable. "Those taste a little better if you heat them up in the microwave for a few seconds."

He was already biting into the hard lump before she completed voicing the suggestion. Tipping his head back as if tasting the most delicious thing in the world, he revealed, "It has been so long since I've had a donut."

"I don't think those are gluten-free, and I know they're not fat-free or organic," Grace informed him.

"You know what?" Dash asked before pausing, as if getting ready to reveal a big secret. "I'm not even sure what gluten is, but I think I like it."

The amount of wonder in his voice made Grace chuckle. Turning to look at her, Dash asked, "Why did I ever give this stuff up?"

She shook her head at the silly man. "I don't know, but I need to go get ready, or I'll be late to work and won't be able to bring you any more free, stale donuts."

"Well, get moving then, woman," he teased her before seeming to turn serious. Lifting the cruller in her direction, he added, "I need these in my life."

When she eased past him in the narrow entryway that connected the kitchen and living room, she caught a whiff of the delicious, pure-male scent that she recognized as his freshly-showered aroma. "See you tonight." Her voice sounded husky, even though that hadn't been her intent.

"Can't wait." He grinned down at her before turning to Star. "Are you ready to go to work?" The high degree of enthusiasm he had inserted into his voice, plus the usage of the word 'go'––one of her favorite buzzwords––had the puppy circling with excitement.

Thrilled to see him making a real effort with the little dog, Grace closed herself into the steamy bathroom and leaned back against the door. "This is *not* a date," she reminded herself quietly.

Despite her best efforts to remember that Dash was being forced to spend time with her, her cheeks hurt from smiling so wide. Her racing pulse and somersaulting tummy didn't seem to want to accept that she did not have a date tonight with the one-and-only Dash Diamond. Her traitorous, illogical heart wanted nothing more than to believe.

22

*G*race was particularly busy at the bakery's counter that morning, so she wasn't able to work in the back during the 9 a.m. hour and watch Dash interact with Star to see if their newfound camaraderie extended to the small screen.

When one of her semi-regular customers, Mrs. Greenwalt, heard the small television echoing out from the kitchen, her face lit up. "Is that *Good Morning Gold Coast*? I've always thought Dash Diamond was the cat's meow." Her rheumy blue eyes lit up as she wiggled her sparse, gray eyebrows up and down.

Grace chuckled and nodded at the sweet, older woman. Before she could tell the woman about Star's lucky break, Mrs. Greenwalt lifted her crooked, arthritic pointer finger. "He better start being nice to that sweet puppy, though, or I'll change the channel and never watch him again." The old woman shook her finger in Grace's direction as she spoke.

"I think he has been trying to bond with her this week," Grace revealed.

Not questioning how Grace knew that, the older

woman's eyes took on a dreamy expression. "Really? I love men who love dogs."

"Me too," Grace added quietly.

Her face lighting up with an idea, Mrs. Greenwalt asked, "Will that television reach around here? Let's watch and see how he gets along with Star today."

Grace wasn't sure about granting the request. She certainly didn't want to get in trouble at work, but it had been the customer who requested the television to be brought out. Would the grocery's policy of 'the customer is always right' extend to watching a tiny television in full view of the store? Looking behind Mrs. Greenwalt and realizing the morning rush was over, Grace made a snap decision to bring the TV out.

Before long, a small crowd was gathered around the tiny set. Grace attempted several times to turn the shoppers' attention back to the store's pastry offerings, but they were only interested in watching Dash and Star. Somehow, the mismatched duo had become the hottest topic in Redwood Cove.

Riveted to the screen, they watched as Dash captivated the camera with his morning spiel. Sitting close by his side, Star nudged his hand with her head in an attempt to get him to pay her some attention.

Normally, Dash would simply fold his hands together or find some other way to ignore the puppy's obvious plea for his attention. Today, though, he reached over and ruffled her soft ears.

Savoring the rare show of affection from him, Star tilted her head up and gazed at the talk show host as if he were a giant T-bone steak. The enamored look the puppy gave him as she rolled over and presented her soft white belly for him to rub was so touching that Grace involuntarily brought her hand up to rest over her heart.

The moment was quickly ruined for her when the mother with the young boy in her cart shook her head and said, "Just when I thought that man couldn't be any hotter."

Grace couldn't explain why the young mom's open admiration of Dash made her blood boil. Of course, she knew Dash was the object of many local women's fantasies, but hearing about it first-hand made her jaw tighten uncomfortably as her teeth clamped together.

She struggled not to comment about the woman saying such a thing in front of her young son, even as she told herself it was absolutely none of her business.

Even the tall, well-dressed young man near the back of the small group weighed in when Dash paused his monologue to rub the puppy's belly and tell her what a good girl she was. "I dare anyone to try to resist that," he said to the gathering of diverse women.

Proving that Dash appealed to all shapes, sizes, and ages, they all giggled in tacit agreement with the man's assessment——even Grace.

By the time the show ended and the small crowd dispersed, Grace felt confident that Dash had nailed his attempt to prove he had bonded with Star.

She firmly tamped down the tiny niggling fear that he was doing all of this merely to save his job, rather than it being a newfound appreciation for her sweet pet. Wanting to give him the benefit of the doubt, she decided if he was that good of an actor, then he needed to move down the coast to Hollywood.

Not wanting the grocery's management to see the television out on the counter, she moved it back to its normal spot in the back. It had been worth the minimal risk of getting caught to get to see Dash interact so lovingly with Star this morning. Besides, she had tried to wait on the customers, but they had been more interested in watching the formerly aloof host warm to the lovable and playful puffball. After watching the show, the shoppers bought baked goods, so Grace silently justified the short break as an effort in building customer goodwill.

As she loaded the bakery's industrial dishwasher, she daydreamed about what her dinner tonight with Dash would be like. The mere thought of him cooking a family recipe in her tiny kitchen made butterflies flutter their wings in her belly. She hoped she wouldn't be too nervous to eat.

Grace decided she was being silly to get so worked up over a simple meal—especially since Dash was *required* to spend time with Star, and therefore her. In an effort to rein in the surge of hope that was nearly overwhelming her, Grace began ticking off on her fingers why the local celebrity should *not* make her heart thump wildly in her chest.

When she got to his frequent use of the third person to describe himself, she threw her hands up in the air—frustrated with herself for even letting the edges of hope for a relationship with Dash to creep into her head. *How could I even consider being with someone who announces his own entry into a room?*

She fought down the urge to defend his obnoxious habit. Even though he had stopped announcing himself to her, it didn't negate the fact that he had deemed it appropriate to do at some point. In fact, he might still do it with others. She tried to envision walking into a party on Dash's arm and having him announce loudly, "Dash Diamond is here!" She would crawl into a hole and die of embarrassment.

She wondered if his over-the-top persona that he put on and took off, like a hat, might be an act that he thought people expected of a big celebrity. The fact that he no longer acted full of himself around her and Clover made her think it might be.

Time would reveal the real Dash Diamond, and Grace

was excited by the prospect. How he behaved during tonight's date would be a good test of his true personality.

Realizing she had called tonight's dinner a 'date'––even if only in her own mind––made Grace's palms feel sweaty, despite the grocery's frigid air. It wasn't a date... was it?

23

*G*race refused to question why she spent extra time getting ready and bothered applying her lash-lengthening mascara for her non-date with Dash. It was just a simple dinner that he happened to be cooking. Besides, Clover would be there. And Star. Their presence automatically put the evening into the non-romantic category, and she intended to make sure it stayed there.

The last thing she needed was to get involved with an egomaniacal celebrity like Dash Diamond. She would have to make sure to remember that when he turned those dazzling blue eyes––that could make her mind turn to mush––in her direction.

When the four of them regrouped at Grace's apartment later that afternoon, it was obvious Dash was in a great mood. "The head honchos at the studio were thrilled with my progress so far in bonding with Star. They said it's paying off in the ratings."

Nodding, Grace told him, "I caught some of the show, and your growing connection with her is really beginning to show."

Dash bent to ruffle the pup's ears. "Who knew simply pretending to like you could skyrocket ratings?"

Grace bristled inwardly at his use of the word, 'pretending,' but she tried not to let it show.

"Let's go for a walk down to the park before dinner," Dash suggested enthusiastically.

His idea made Clover's eyes light up with excitement. "Can we, Mama? Pleeease." Normally, Grace didn't appreciate it when Clover took on that somewhat whiny, begging tone. Seeing the puppy whirl around with glee as two of her favorite people donned tennis shoes in anticipation of Grace's agreement made it impossible for her to say no.

The foursome couldn't walk more than a few feet at a time without someone stopping them to request a signature from Dash, a snuggle from Star, or a selfie with both of them.

Grace wondered if it bothered Clover to have the other two get all of the attention. She leaned down to whisper in her daughter's ear, "I guess we're chopped liver, huh?"

Clover wrinkled her nose in distaste at the thought of liver before saying logically, "They are television celebrities."

With that, their roles were accepted, and they carried on their stop-and-go walk. When Grace was handed a cell phone to snap a picture of a stranger with Dash and Star for the tenth time, she began to embrace her unofficial job as their photographer.

She enjoyed watching the strangers' faces light up when she would enthuse, "Beautiful!" or "Love that smile!"

By the time they reached the park, Grace was ready for the stuttering stop-and-go nature of their walk to be over. She wondered if this was how her life would be from now on when she took Star out in public. Clover was adorable and got lots of kind words and smiles from strangers, but nothing like this level of attention.

Due to the relaxed nature of the morning show, it was

almost as if people felt like they knew the host and puppy. They greeted them like old friends, even though they had never actually met Dash or Star.

Dash handled the attention like a champ. He was obviously used to being the center of attention wherever he went. For her part, Star seemed to preen and enjoy the interest her newfound fame drew as well.

Clover ran off to make some new friends on the playground equipment, and a small crowd gathered around Dash and Star. Dash was holding the puppy's leash, so it wasn't long before Grace was pushed out of their vicinity.

Grace quietly made her way over to sit on a bench to keep an eye on Clover as people excitedly asked Dash incredibly personal questions––which he smoothly brushed off––and fawned over Star, who sat still like a regal queen greeting her minions.

Dash made eye contact with Grace over the crowd. His questioning gaze seemed to be asking her if she was okay with being left out of their growing circle of admiration. She gave him what she hoped was a reassuring smile and pointed to the playground to let him know she needed to watch Clover. He nodded his understanding before returning his attention back to his adoring fans.

It was a long time before the crowd around Dash and Star began to disband. Clover was thrilled to have extra playtime, but the bench was hard beneath Grace's rear end and her stomach was beginning to growl. She was ready to go home, but she didn't want to ruin what might be the one chance some of these people would ever get to interact with their favorite morning show celebrities.

When she leaned forward and shifted her weight to the other side, trying to find a comfortable position on the bench, Dash's gaze immediately turned in her direction. It almost seemed like he had been using some sixth-sense to monitor her mood. Evidently sensing she was ready to go, he kindly, yet firmly told the mostly-female group around him that he was leaving.

Aside from some murmurs of disappointment, his fans let him go. They seemed to understand that he had been generous with his time, but now he was done.

Dash and Star approached Grace's bench. "Ready to go?" he asked her, not seeming to hold any ill-will towards her for breaking up his circle of fan worship.

She supposed it was nothing special for him to get rushed by adoring fans. It probably happened everywhere he went. Nodding, she answered his question, "I am, but Clover probably isn't. She's never ready to leave the park."

"I'll take care of it," he promised, walking confidently towards the monkey bars.

Grace had serious doubts about that, so she was stunned when Dash whispered something in Clover's ear, which made her nod, wave goodbye to her new friends, and bound towards the bench where her mother was seated.

Dash handed off Star's leash to Clover, and they let the two young ones lead the way home. The air was quickly cooling off as the sun began to set. With the approach of evening, a brisk wind had kicked up that had Grace folding her arms under her chest in an attempt to keep warm.

She wished she had thought to grab a jacket, but she hadn't anticipated being gone this long on a simple walk to the park. Clover seemed perfectly fine as she skipped along ahead of them with Star. The little girl's bright red cheeks had been a clear indication to Grace that she had gotten overly warm as she played on the playground equipment, so the chilly breeze was probably refreshing to her.

Proving he wasn't completely self-absorbed, Dash said to Grace, "You look cold." With that simple statement, he wrapped a warm arm around her shoulders.

He didn't have on long sleeves either, but being so close to the side of his body was like being enveloped by a heated electric blanket. She sank into the soothing warmth of his embrace. "You're so warm." She looked up into his eyes and tried to justify snuggling with him, even as she noticed the undeniable tingle at being so close to him.

He nodded. "I know when I'm being used simply for body heat, but I'm okay with it." His eyes sparkled down at her to let her know he wasn't angry that she was 'using' him.

She was tempted to reveal to him that the warmth was nice, but that having his arm around her would feel marvelous even when she wasn't cold. Deciding that would be too flirtatious––especially since the man was simply making the best of a situation where he was forced to spend time with her––she remained quiet on the subject.

When they reached the cliff walk that curved between the picturesque oceanfront homes, high above the water, Clover turned to ask if they could take the scenic route. "It's kind of chilly," Grace hedged. She would be glad to enjoy the extra time walking with Dash's arm around her, but she wasn't sure if he was too cold or tired.

"I'm game if you are," he answered jovially. "I've never been up there."

"What?" Clover asked him, stunned. "We love it up there."

"You're in for a treat," Grace assured him. "We sometimes even see orcas breaching in the distance."

"Really?" He sounded truly enthusiastic.

When they reached the highest point of the cliff, they stopped for a moment to catch their breath and enjoy the amazing view.

"No orcas today, I guess." Dash sounded truly disappointed, until he brightened with an idea. "Maybe we can go on one of those whale watching tours that operates out of the harbor one of these days."

Clover's eyes looked like they might pop out of her head from excitement. "Can we, Mama?"

"That sounds like a terrific idea," Grace nodded. At that, Clover turned and skipped with Star down the path towards home.

Grace and Dash exchanged a smile before following her. It felt good to have tentative plans for an outing together.

Changing gears, Grace asked, "What did you say to Clover to get her to leave the park so willingly? I need you to teach me that trick for when you're no longer around." She had meant for the change in topic to maintain the light-hearted and fun tone, but blurting aloud that his time with them was temporary made her face turn down involuntarily.

Not seeming to notice the sudden shift, Dash's voice held a teasing tone when he said, "That's a secret between me and Clover."

Grace hadn't realized Clover was listening to them, so she was surprised when the little girl stopped skipping and turned back to say to Dash, "Don't tell her."

"No way," he answered her. "That's our special secret."

The two of them shared a significant moment, which left Grace feeling aghast. She looked back and forth between them, not quite able to believe they had forged some secret bond that omitted her. Deciding to play along, she teased them, "I'll get one of you to break."

She sounded more confident in that assertion than she felt. It was a strange sensation to have her little girl sharing secrets with anyone but her. She wasn't sure she liked it–– especially since Dash was a temporary fixture in their lives. If he had been staying permanently, it would have warmed her heart to see their relationship flourishing, but as it was, it filled her with a vague, yet very real, sense of concern and dread.

"Never!" Clover yelled in answer to Grace's implied challenge. The little girl's eyes were flashing with excitement as she looked to Dash for backup.

"My lips are sealed," he promised, making a zipping motion across them with his free hand.

The child giggled with glee, thrilled to have a secret from her mom. It made Grace's heart flutter to see Clover so happy. She had given up long ago on finding a father figure for her daughter, outside of Marlene's perpetually gloomy husband, Dan.

She knew it wasn't a possibility with Dash because he was a much sought-after and self-centered bachelor celebrity, but for the first time in years, Grace wondered if she should open her heart up to finding a dad for Clover… and a husband for herself.

Even though she knew he couldn't possibly sense what she was thinking, Dash tightened his arm ever-so-slightly around Grace, pulling her into an even more delightful embrace. Smiling to herself, Grace decided she could get used to that secure feeling––just not with Dash Diamond.

24

*G*race didn't know what to expect from Dash's plan to cook dinner, but his skills in the kitchen went way above and beyond anything she could have imagined.

He insisted that she not lift a finger to help, so she sat at the table sipping the fruity, delicious glass of Pinot Noir he had poured for her. After glancing at the label on the bottle to confirm her suspicion, she said, "Dorma Valley Wine is the best. The woman who owns the vineyard comes to the grocery where I work. She brought me a bottle once, and I've been hooked on it ever since."

"It's my favorite, too," he commented as he tipped the pot of steaming spaghetti into the colander in the sink.

Grace couldn't help but be impressed by his choice of wine. She would have assumed that he would have more expensive, pretentious taste.

Once he plated their food, Grace eyed her meal appreciatively. She was delighted to discover that the pasta noodles were perfectly al dente, the cheesy garlic bread was browned just right, and his homemade mouth-watering red sauce...

she couldn't even find the words to describe the explosion of marvelous flavors bursting in her mouth.

As she chewed the first bite, Dash sat on the edge of his seat and waited for her verdict. "Well?!?" He was obviously impatient to hear what she thought.

She gave him a 'mouth's full' signal to request a moment before speaking. Clover had a bite of spaghetti in her mouth, too, but she gave him two enthusiastic thumbs up of non-verbal approval.

When Grace finally swallowed, she gave Dash her opinion. "So good!" She infused her voice with enthusiasm because it truly was delicious.

"Really?" He sought further confirmation, even though he had already sagged back into his chair with relief at her initial reaction.

She only nodded to confirm because she was already greedily shoveling the next bite into her mouth.

Evidently appeased by her approval, Dash tucked into his own plate. The trio ate in silence for a bit, until Clover loudly sucked a long noodle into her mouth that slapped sauce up onto her nose on its way in.

Grace attempted to hide her flash of embarrassment over her child's suddenly uncouth manners. It wasn't unusual for them to act silly like that when they were home alone, but she would have expected Clover to behave more civilized in front of company.

The table was silent for a moment as Clover smiled happily at her trick, Grace tried to think of an excuse for her daughter's poor manners, and Dash gawked at them both. It seemed like an interminable amount of time until Dash reached over with his napkin to swipe it across Clover's nose. "It's hard to take you seriously when you have a red nose, Rudolph."

The child giggled, but Grace was still uncertain if their

in-house celebrity was appalled by Clover's momentary lapse in table manners, until he took a bite from his own plate and slurped his pasta like Clover had. That broke the ice, and soon they were all sucking the noodles like hooligans and laughing hysterically.

It felt so much like a joyous family moment, Grace had to remind herself it was merely an illusion. It would have been too easy to slip into the fantasy that she and Dash were a happy couple, raising Clover together.

When they were finished eating, Grace dared to turn her head to look at the mess in the kitchen. It appeared Dash had used every pot, pan, and dish in her kitchen to make the meal. "Time to clean up this mess." She couldn't hide the dread in her voice over facing her least-favorite household chore.

"We'll help, won't we?" Dash turned to Clover, who nodded enthusiastically.

Grace knew from experience that Clover's 'help' ended up making chores take three times as long. "You made dinner," she reminded Dash. "It wouldn't be fair to put you on cleanup duty, too." She let him off the hook, even though she was touched by his kind offer.

Not accepting her reprieve, Dash jumped up and carried their plates the few steps into the kitchen. Clover followed his lead and dragged a chair over to the sink to begin washing the dishes. For her part, Star plopped down right beside Clover's chair, right in the way.

Deciding she would probably need to re-wash the dishes later to get them truly clean, but thrilled to see her daughter so willing to help out, Grace set about putting the leftover sauce into a container so they could reheat it later in the week.

"How long has it been since you've done dishes?" She

turned an ornery grin in Dash's direction, suspecting it had been longer than he would want to admit.

"A while," Dash answered cryptically, confirming her suspicion.

Deciding to tease him a little, she added, "You have 'people' for that, right?"

"It's fun to pretend to be a commoner once in a while." His lighthearted tone didn't hold a trace of the obnoxious, entitled celebrity persona he occasionally adopted.

After a pause, Clover changed the subject by piping up to ask the man, "What kind of name is Dash Diamond, anyway?"

Grace coughed, almost choking from embarrassment. It wasn't like her child to be so bold, bordering on rude. She hoped Dash wouldn't take offense to the brash question.

Leaning down as if revealing a great secret, Dash said to the little girl, "It's actually just my stage name."

Her blue eyes widening with intrigue, Clover asked him, "What's your real name?" Grace couldn't deny that she was leaning in, desperate to know the answer as well.

Both mother and daughter stopped their activity with the dishes as they anxiously awaited his response. He seemed to consider it for a moment, but then said, "It's a secret."

Clover made a sound of disappointment, but Dash refused to budge. "Only my family and a few close friends know what it is, and they'll never tell."

"We could be your new family, right, Mama?" Her hopeful gaze shot up at Grace.

Dash saved her from having to answer the awkward question by hedging, "Maybe one of these days I'll tell you, but you have to prove yourself to be a master secret keeper."

"I am." Clover nodded solemnly, her eyes wide with sincerity.

"You wouldn't tell even if you were tortured by tickling?"

Dash lightly tickled the little girl's side, making her squeal with giggles.

"No, I would never-ever tell anyone," Clover promised him when he stopped.

He merely nodded in answer as if he was taking her loyalty under duress into account.

Grace hoped if Dash did end up revealing his real name to Clover that he would tell her, too. She wasn't sure why, but it felt important for her to be in the man's trusted inner circle.

They worked in companionable silence until Dash rolled the dish towel he was holding and playfully flipped it in Grace's direction.

She turned wide eyes at him, not quite able to believe what had just happened. "Oh, no you didn't!"

"Oh... I think I did." He nodded and gave her a cocky grin.

Clover had stopped cleaning dishes and was turned to look at them, giggling joyfully.

Not wanting to be outdone, Grace leaped forward and grabbed the sink's spray nozzle. Pointing it in Dash's direction, she pulled the trigger and water sprayed out over him and her kitchen floor.

Not used to seeing her mom act so silly, Clover squealed in surprise. Star jumped into the fun and tried to bite at the spraying water. Dash reacted quickly to being doused with water. He went for the flexible hose. They struggled over it, spraying water from floor to ceiling, and before long, they were all four soaked and the humans were laughing hysterically.

It was a carefree moment of fun and complete abandon. Grace couldn't help but wonder if this was how their lives would be with a man in their family—not the almighty Dash Diamond, of course, but a regular guy who would accept Clover as his own daughter and help Grace raise her.

Grace had been the head of their little household long enough that she knew she could handle the big things life threw at them on her own, but she couldn't deny that having someone by her side for the day-to-day living would sure be pleasant. This little taste of having a man in their space was making her crave something she hadn't realized she missed.

Once the cleanup of the dishes and the sopping up of their water mess was complete, it was Dash who piped up with the suggestion that they play a game. "When I was little, we used to play a card game called Uno. Have you ever heard of it?"

Clover's eyes lit up. "We love Uno!" She was already running to retrieve their big stack of Uno cards.

Their game turned rowdy when Dash got down to one card but forgot to say, "Uno."

"Can't you give me a pass just this once?" he whined when Clover called him out on it.

"Nope, that's the rules." Clover held firm, but looked to her Mom for confirmation. Grace nodded her agreement, so Dash reluctantly drew additional cards.

Clover ended up winning the lively game fair and square, which made her do an exuberant happy-dance. Star jumped and twirled her little body around, trying to join in the festivities.

Grace made them chocolate and banana milkshakes to celebrate Clover's win. She smiled as she put a scoop of vanilla into a dish for Star. Dash had remembered the puppy's vanilla ice cream when he bought the other ingredients for their dinner. Once she was done, they settled in with their desserts to watch the little girl's favorite singing competition television show.

The trio shared a blanket and slurped their milkshakes as

Star--who had scarfed down her vanilla treat within seconds--rested at their feet and chewed on one of her many toys. While Clover and Dash bickered about which young singer should win, Grace couldn't help but think how quickly Dash had assimilated himself into their family and how pleasant it was to have him there.

Mimicking her thoughts, Dash turned during a commercial break and looked over Clover's head at her. "A man could get used to this."

Happy warmth flooded her system, and Grace could feel the walls she had carefully built around her heart beginning to crumble. Steeling her will, she firmly reminded herself that Dash didn't have a choice about being here and that playing house with him was very temporary. Soon enough, he would go back to his real life as a pampered and spoiled celebrity. He probably wouldn't give them another thought after that.

When the show returned, she stole a glance at Dash out of the corner of her eye. Sighing quietly, she decided that keeping him at arm's length would be much simpler if he wasn't so handsome, charming, and irresistible. This week needed to quickly come to an end before she completely fell for the blasted man.

25

*T*he next morning, instead of silently fuming about Dash's lengthy bathroom routine, Grace set her alarm thirty minutes early. She would be able to be in and out of the shower before Dash got up. Besides, the allure of her newly installed towel warmer was calling to her. As much as she hated to admit that she liked the luxurious treat of heated towels, she wasn't sure how she had lived without it for so long, and she never intended to deny herself of it again. She didn't even bother to question when Dash's handy man had sneaked in to install it.

Deciding the minor inconvenience of getting up extra early would be temporary, she used the extra time to read a few chapters of a delightful and funny romance novel after her shower. She rarely made the time to read, even though she thoroughly enjoyed it and considered it time well spent.

With Grace's modified schedule, their morning routine somehow slipped into a well-oiled machine. Each person knew the schedule and timelines. Even Star seemed to understand what needed to happen and when. The eager-to-please puppy did her part to help with the early-morning rush.

When Grace dropped Clover off at Marlene's, the woman gave her a knowing smile. "It sounded like you all were having fun last night."

"We had a serious game of Uno going." Grace looked down at the counter and smiled at the memory. Suddenly concerned that they might have been too rambunctious for their thin, shared walls, she turned to her landlord and friend. "Did we bother you?"

"Like it could ever bother me hearing two of my favorite people having so much fun," Marlene reassured her. Turning serious, the woman added, "Just be careful, okay."

Her implied meaning came through to Grace loud and clear. Her friend was warning her not to get too attached to what would most definitely be a short-term fixture in their lives. "I know he won't stick around once the studio execs let him off the hook." Grace tried to infuse her tone with certainty, even though her heart desperately wanted to let her forget that having Dash as part of their family was temporary.

"It's fun having him around," she admitted, "But he's not the right man for us."

Marlene nodded, obviously assessing Grace's sincerity. "I just don't want you to get hurt." She reached over to place a comforting hand on Grace's.

"I know." Grace nodded before adding, "And we won't."

She wished she felt half as confident as she sounded. One of her main concerns was that Clover was already becoming too attached to having Dash in their lives, but they were in too deep to turn back now.

"We're keeping things light and casual," she promised, trying to insert the appropriate amount of levity in her voice.

"Besides, Clover is having a blast beating him at every game under the sun."

With that, Grace walked over to the table where Clover was eating breakfast with Marlene's kids. After a quick kiss goodbye for her daughter, she waved to Marlene and bolted out the door, not wanting the other woman to question her any more about her growing attachment to Dash Diamond.

The bakery was hopping that morning, so Grace wasn't able to keep an eye on the show. She normally liked to at least check in on what was happening with Star and Dash, but with so many customers, it simply wasn't an option.

When she looked up after the morning rush, she was shocked to find that it was already almost eleven. Not only had she missed the show, she had also not had a chance to clean up the back kitchen for the afternoon crew. She preferred to have things spic and span for them to begin their shift with a freshly cleaned workspace.

The high-pitched trilling of her cell phone from her pink uniform's pocket startled her. She rarely received phone calls, and she technically wasn't supposed to have her phone on her at work, but she wasn't willing to be too far from it, in case Clover's school needed to reach her.

She recognized the television studio's prefix on the incoming call number. Taking a deep breath, she answered, while silently praying that Star hadn't destroyed the set or pulled some other ornery trick during today's show.

"Hello?" Trepidation filled her voice. Calls so far from the studio hadn't been good news.

"Grace, it's Evelyn." The normally brisk woman sounded especially frazzled. Her voice held an urgency that put Grace on immediate high alert. Without waiting for Grace to greet her, Evelyn rushed on. "Star is missing."

Of all the possible scenarios that had raced through Grace's mind, this wasn't one of them. "What do you mean she's missing?" She struggled to comprehend the woman's words.

"Did she run away? Send someone out to find her." Her voice sounded screechy near the end of her outburst. All she could picture in her mind was Clover's devastated expression when she learned their beloved puppy was missing.

Trying to calm her jittery nerves, Grace took a deep breath. "She can't have gone far. Have everyone stop what they're doing and look for her." This assertive side of Grace tended to emerge when she went into mama-bear mode. Star was ingrained into their family, so the thought of losing her made Grace's stomach feel queasy.

Grace ran around the grocery with her phone held to her ear as she grabbed her purse, clocked out, and searched for the manager-on-duty to fill in at her post. It dawned on her then that Evelyn had been oddly quiet. Pausing in her frantic action, she ran a hand through her hair before asking, "What is it?"

The woman hesitated on the other end of the phone. She was obviously not anxious to share whatever she had to say. When she spoke, her voice sounded softer than normal. "We don't think she ran away. You better come down to the studio, and we'll explain everything."

"Didn't run away…" Grace mumbled, trying to comprehend what the woman was insinuating. Her mind felt like it was slogging through Jell-O as she tried to make sense of what she was hearing. When it clicked into place, she screeched, "You mean someone took her?!?"

"Just come down to the studio," Evelyn said before hanging up.

Grace stared at her phone's blank screen. Unshed tears

and fear-laced dread clogged her throat as the painful truth sank in. Someone had taken their sweet puppy.

26

The studio was bustling with a flurry of activity, even though the crew didn't seem to know exactly what they were supposed to be doing. Grace watched them run from one thing to the next like ants on speed. Their faces were drawn with worry, and no one seemed to be willing to make eye contact with her––despite their welcoming friendliness during her last few visits. The shift made her nausea kick into high gear.

Miles was the first person to speak to her. "Grace, let's get you settled upstairs in the conference room."

His slick, seemingly calm demeanor made Grace more agitated. "No! We need to be looking for Star!" She yanked her elbow out of his grasp when he tried to steer her in the direction of the stairs.

"We have people on it," he promised before adding, "Come upstairs and we'll explain everything."

Not seeing a better alternative, Grace reluctantly went up to the conference room. She was surprised to find all of the bigwigs and studio management already assembled. They had been talking loudly. A man she didn't recognize was gesturing wildly, waving his arms around, but silence reigned when she entered the room and sat down at the enormous table.

All eyes stared at her as if they expected her to lead this charge. Clearing her throat, she asked her most pressing question, "What are we doing to find Star?"

Rather than answering, the head honcho leaned forward to pass a paper in her direction. "You should have a look at this." His voice sounded even more deep and somber than normal.

Once the people between them had handed it off, the mysterious paper finally reached her. Grace was startled to see that it was a classic ransom note with letters cut out from magazines. She had never seen anything like it, except on television.

She quickly scanned the note, which read in mismatched letters, *I have the Star of your show. The ransom is 1 mil.*

Grace's first wayward thought was that this idiot was asking for a million dollars, but couldn't be bothered to find all the letters to spell out the entire word. As soon as her brain started functioning properly again, she realized she should be focusing on getting Star back, rather than the moron that took her.

"Have you shown this to the police? Are they out looking for her? Do you have any idea who is behind this? Are you pulling together the ransom money to get her back?" The questions rushed out in a flurry as the eyes around the table merely blinked back at her.

As she searched the blank faces, she suddenly craved Dash's calm, confident presence. After a quick scan of the group, she confirmed her suspicion that he wasn't in the room. "Where is Dash? He needs to be included in this."

"Well, that's the thing…" the studio president splayed his hands in her direction. "Dash seems to be missing, too."

A vice grip squeezed around Grace's heart--she was certain of it. "What?!?" she managed to croak, even as her eyes darted back to the ransom note. It read, *I have the Star of your show.*

Shooting her gaze back at the president, who seemed to be the only one willing or able to answer her questions. "So, do they have Star or Dash?" Her heart sank even further towards her stomach as she asked, "Or both?"

For the first time, the studio exec showed a chink in his armor by glancing at the man to his left. Evidently not finding the answer he needed, the powerful man finally admitted, "We're not exactly sure."

Outrage immediately surged through Grace. She slammed her palms on the glossy mahogany table. "Not sure! How can you not be sure?!?" Even though she knew it wasn't the executive's fault, she wasn't feeling overly rational as she faced the fear that Star and Dash might have both been abducted.

Miles slithered into his smooth producer role. "We know Star is missing. Dash was seen willingly leaving the studio with chef Emily Hart after this morning's show. I would imagine they are continuing this morning's spicy cooking segment at her place, if you know what I mean." He waggled his eyebrows to enunciate his naughty insinuation before continuing, "So, no one can blame him for not answering his cell while he's otherwise occupied."

Miles' not-at-all subtle suggestion about Dash's whereabouts came through loud and clear. Grace's stomach churned as if she might be violently ill. She shut her eyes and tried to block the mental image of Dash with the beautiful chef, who had become such a fan favorite that the producers had decided she would have a weekly segment on the show.

Grace had seen their openly flirtatious banter many times on the show, but had assumed it was all an act for the camera. It didn't make sense for her to be so affected by the knowledge that the two of them had an off-camera relationship, so she told herself it was merely a delayed reaction over her worry about Star.

Wanting to change gears back to her missing puppy, Grace said, "So, Dash is probably perfectly fine. We need to focus on getting Star safely back home. Who had access to her after the show?"

After some raucous conversation and finger pointing, it was obvious that anyone from the staff, crew, or studio audience could have puppy-napped Star.

Grace used her loud voice to announce, "Okay, so from now on... everyone is considered a suspect."

Dash Diamond chose that moment to burst into the conference room.

27

*D*ash perused the crowd in the room before asking, "Having a show-planning meeting without Dash Diamond?"

Grace bristled when she realized he had slipped back into his obnoxious persona that liked to refer to himself in the third person. This celebrity was so different from the fun-loving man that fully participated in the water spray fight at her kitchen sink and slurped spaghetti with her daughter.

She wondered which version of Dash was the real one. Was the laid-back, easy-going man she thought she knew just an act? When the idea dawned on her, she sucked in a sharp breath. *What if he still secretly hated Star and wanted her off the show and out of his life?* There was no denying that one of Dash's personalities was a fake, and she needed to know which one.

Her voice rang out clear when she asked him, "Did you arrange to have Star puppy-napped?"

Silence reigned in the conference room as all eyes stared at Dash, waiting to see how he would react to the accusatory question.

Dash looked at Grace as if he was unaware that anyone else was in the room. The shocked, hurt expression on his face was undeniable. "Puppy-napped?" he finally asked. "Star is missing?"

If he was acting, he was doing an Oscar-worthy job of it. The eyes in the room volleyed to Grace as if they were watching a riveting tennis match.

"We all know you don't really like her and that you'd do anything to get her off the show." Grace defended her bold allegation.

Dash's face fell. "You think that little of me?" His voice sounded small and very un-Dash Diamond-like. As if suddenly realizing the full implications of the conversation, he asked, "Where is Star? Why isn't everyone out looking for her? We need to bring her home."

The true concern evident in his tone alleviated Grace's fear that he might have been involved in Star's disappearance. A tidal wave of guilt washed over her for jumping to incorrect conclusions about him. Deciding they needed to focus on the most urgent matter at hand, she slid the ransom note in Dash's direction.

He shook his head as he read it, as if he almost couldn't believe what his eyes were telling him. "I have the Star of your show," he mumbled almost to himself.

Grace felt certain he was going to balk at the puppy-napper's reference to Star as being the star of his show, so she was impressed when he didn't.

"Okay." He looked up to the room at large as he processed the words, searching for clues. "It's obviously someone working alone because he used the word 'I' rather than 'we.'"

Grace liked where Dash was heading with this. He seemed to be the only one willing to work through this in a logical manner to help find Star. Leaning forward to look at the note again, she said excitedly, "His use of 'your show' implies he isn't directly involved in the show, or he would have used the word 'our' instead."

"Yes!" Dash beamed at her, and they shared a moment of quiet triumph before Dash switched into his role as a take-charge celebrity.

"You." He pointed at one of the men in suits across the table. "Call the police department to get them working on this case and have them analyze this ransom note for clues."

The man nodded, looking relieved to have a clear job to accomplish.

"Evelyn!" Dash called out, which made the mousy woman jump.

"Yes?" she asked sheepishly before scribbling furiously on her clipboard as Dash listed off her jobs of contacting each member of the studio audience to see if they saw anything, making flyers to hang around town, and starting a social media campaign on his Reel Life account to spread the word that Star was missing.

"Let's go downstairs and film a promo spot that can air day and night until Star is home. We'll have all of Redwood Cove looking for that puppy." His enthusiasm infused the room with a confidence they had lacked before Dash's arrival.

Grace couldn't deny being impressed by his collected presence and firm leadership of the group. As they filed out of the room, she held back, hoping to speak to Dash privately.

When they were the last two in the room, he turned on her. The look of devastation on his face was gut wrenching. "How could you think I would do this?" he asked her, before adding, "I thought you knew me better than that."

Grace wasn't sure what to say. She hated the feeling of

having hurt Dash's feelings, but in her defense, she wasn't sure if the Dash she knew was the real man.

Before she could formulate an appropriate response, he said, "We have a puppy to find." With that, he stalked out of the room, leaving her feeling like a complete heel.

28

*D*ash gave a poignant, pleading appeal for anyone who knew anything about Star's whereabouts to contact the hotline that had hastily been set up. The 30-second spot was scheduled to begin airing immediately, and Grace knew Star's disappearance would soon be the hot topic the entire Gold Coast was talking about.

Not wanting Clover to hear about it from someone else, Grace bolted to the elementary school to pick up her little girl.

Clover's lip quivered when Grace told her about Star's puppy-napping. "We have to get her back, Mama." Crocodile-sized tears were forming in the little girl's lower lids.

"We will," Grace assured her, praying she was right.

"Where is Dash? We need him." With those simple words, Grace realized her little girl was already completely attached to the exasperating man.

There was no denying the distraught feeling of a gaping, burning hole in her own heart as it ached from having accused and hurt him. Somehow, the pompous celebrity had weaseled his way into an integral spot in their little family.

Pursing her lips, Grace reminded herself that Dash hadn't been at the studio when Star was stolen because he was off cavorting with the beautiful and talented chef, Emily Hart. He didn't want the place they had created for him in their lives.

"He's not coming, sweetheart," she said gently, unwilling to get into the smarmy details with the child.

She wouldn't have believed it to be possible, but Clover's face looked even more crestfallen than it had at the news of Star's disappearance.

Nodding sadly to accept the revelation about Dash, Clover told her mom solemnly, "We need to look for her." Her eyes lighting up with an idea, Clover said, "I can make flyers to hang up around town. I'll even draw a picture of her, so people know what she looks like."

Grace figured nearly everyone knew what the famous little puppy looked like, but she didn't want to disappoint her child any further. "Great idea." She tried to insert some enthusiasm into her voice. Even though the studio had posted flyers and much of the town was already looking for Star, she figured they needed to do their part as well. Besides, they needed to keep busy to avoid sitting around and moping about the loss of two of their household members.

Clover and Marlene's kids worked tirelessly on hand-drawn pictures of Star with Grace's cell phone number and a request for any information on her whereabouts written in large, block print. The letters angled upward and got smaller towards the end, as signs made by children tend to do.

"These are terrific," Grace told them honestly as she inspected the signs. "They will attract a lot of attention." She put an arm around Clover to give her a reassuring squeeze.

"I just know they'll work. I can't wait for Star to come home!" Clover seemed confident.

Grace gave Marlene a concerned look over the kids'

heads. She knew the longer they went without finding Star and bringing her safely home, the less likely it was they would end up with a good outcome. It didn't feel right to let her daughter grasp onto false hopes, but she couldn't stand to break her heart by discussing any of the less appealing alternatives.

At some point, if Star wasn't found, she knew she'd need to have a tough conversation with the little girl. She doubted if the studio would pay the million-dollar ransom, and Grace didn't have the money to even give her the option of paying it, so the only way this could work out in their favor was if the culprit was discovered and brought to justice before any harm could befall their innocent little puppy.

The look Marlene gave back to Grace was somber, but the woman slowly nodded her head. The silent agreement that Marlene felt she was handling this appropriately made Grace sag with relief. They would have to take it day-by-day, but for now, she had confidence in her decision to let Clover remain hopeful for Star's swift and safe return.

"Let's go hang these signs," she suggested to Clover as she kissed the top of her little girl's head.

Ever helpful, Marlene had a canvas bag with a hammer and nails, an industrial-sized stapler, tape, and pushpins ready for them. When she handed the well-stocked bag to Grace, the two women embraced. "You're doing a good job," Marlene whispered reassuringly in her ear as she patted her back.

Tears formed in her eyes, but Grace refused to let them fall in front of her daughter. Instead, she said to Marlene, "We're so lucky to have you."

As they headed out the door, Grace heard Marlene yell at their backs, "We're the lucky ones to have found you two lovely ladies."

Smiling with renewed confidence and hope, Grace and

Clover plastered Redwood Cove with flyers about their missing puppy. By the time they had them all hung, dark and ominous-looking clouds had moved in from the water, and it started misting rain.

Grace turned to her daughter. "Should we splurge for a ride or walk in the rain?"

"We won't melt." Clover grinned up at her as they set off towards home, arm in arm.

When they reached their block, the light mist turned into a downpour of big, pelting raindrops. They ran the last stretch of sidewalk towards their house, but they still got drenched.

"We look like wet rats!" Grace commented once they were safely inside.

"I feel like a wet rat," Clover answered before shaking her head, like she had seen her puppy do after playing in the hose stream. Drops of water sprayed in every direction.

Grace couldn't help but wonder... if they actually lived with Dash, would it have bothered him to have his belongings get all wet from Clover's playful shake? She wasn't sure of the answer to that question. The playful Dash who joyfully joined in their silly antics wouldn't care, but the Dash Diamond celebrity television host she glimpsed at the studio would pitch a fit. Sighing, she realized it would be nice to know which version of the man was real. *Will the real Dash Diamond please step forward?*

Reminding herself she didn't have to worry about it, she suggested to Clover, "How about if we dry off, put on our jammies, and make popcorn with peanut M&M's and hot cocoa for dinner?"

The little girl's eyes lit up as Grace had suspected they would. "Really?" At her mom's confirming nod, she asked, "Can we add whipped cream and sprinkles to our hot chocolate?"

"Sure," Grace couldn't help but smile as her daughter squealed with delight and bolted for her room to dry off and change. Telling herself it was nice to be able to make decisions like that without having anyone else there to judge her, Grace went to her own room to change.

Once they were both in comfy PJ's, they set about making their not-so-nutritious dinner. Clover wanted to help, so it took twice as long and made triple the mess, but Grace enjoyed their easy camaraderie in the kitchen.

Deciding tonight was the perfect night to break all the rules, they settled on the couch in front of the television with their bowls and mugs. They flipped through the kids' movies on their on-demand selections and finally landed on a Disney movie they both agreed on.

As they were getting to the good part of the movie, a knock rapped on their door, startling them both. Clover jumped enough that a few pieces of popcorn popped out of her bowl and landed on her lap.

As a single Mom, Grace was extremely cautious about opening her front door to strangers. She already knew it wasn't any of Marlene's family because they all used the classic rapping rhythm *Shave and a Haircut*, to which Clover would respond with *Two bits* before swinging the door open for them. Clover had learned that simple melody even before she could talk.

This knock was more urgent than a solicitor's would be. Besides, Grace couldn't imagine anyone wanting to sell something badly enough to come out this late at night in the pouring rain.

Proving the person on the other side of the door was impatient as well, the knock sounded again before Grace could pause their show and walk across the living room. Peering cautiously out the peephole, Grace almost couldn't believe her eyes.

"Dash." She sighed with relief.

29

*S*he swung the door wide open. That was when she realized he was soaked to the bone. "Dash!" She almost couldn't believe her eyes as she ushered him inside the warm, dry safety of her home. It was shocking to see the normally perfectly-coiffed celebrity so drenched.

"Clover, go grab some towels, please." As an afterthought, she added with a smile in Dash's direction, "The heated ones."

Once they had him reasonably dried off, Grace made him a mug of hot cocoa to help him warm up. After he was settled on the sofa with the steaming beverage and a soft quilt wrapped around his shoulders, Grace and Clover sat on either side of him.

"What happened? Why were you out in the rain? What have you been doing?" Grace couldn't seem to slow her rapid-fire questions. She wanted all the answers now.

"I was out looking for Star and hanging up fliers," he told them simply.

Grace's heart swelled inside her chest, even as she felt

ashamed for having wondered if he might have been behind Star's abduction.

"I went by the police station," he went on, oblivious to Grace's inner turmoil. "They don't yet have any solid leads, despite hundreds of calls to the hotline with supposed tips. People keep calling to express their love for Star, but they don't know anything about her whereabouts."

Grace nodded. She figured every kind-hearted soul in the area, plus all the loons who were looking for a platform to share their conspiracy theories, would be calling in.

"I checked in with the studio, too," Dash told them. "No real news there, either."

"It sounds like we're doing everything we can," Grace weighed in logically. "Now we wait and let the system work."

"I'm sorry for showing up at your door like this, but I didn't want to go back to my big, empty apartment, and I didn't know where else to go." Dash was looking down at his folded hands. He looked so vulnerable, Grace's heart nearly melted into a puddle.

"You're always welcome here," she reassured him.

The hope-filled gaze he turned on her made her heart flutter. "Really?" he asked.

"Of course." She smiled at him, wanting him to know that her house was a safe place for him, away from the prying eyes of his adoring fans.

Changing subjects, Dash eyed the remains of Clover's bowl of popcorn and M&M's. "I'm starving, and that looks delicious. Can I have some?"

Embarrassed by their childish and simple dinner, Grace offered, "Oh, I can make you something else."

"I'd like to try that." He angled his head at Clover's bowl before adding, "If you have more."

"Sure," Grace answered, jumping up to make another batch of microwavable popcorn.

When she handed him the filled bowl, he ate a handful of the treat before weighing in. "Salty and sweet... perfection!" He enunciated his words by bringing his thumb, index, and middle finger to his lips for a loud kiss in the classic gesture for delicious food.

Glancing at the television screen, he realized they had been in the middle of something. "What are we watching?"

Grace answered, "It's just a kids' movie," before quickly offering, "We can watch something else." Guilt rose in her throat over Clover's crestfallen expression. *Why was she offering to change their life to accommodate Dash?*

He saved her from having to explore that particular realization any further by saying, "I love Disney movies. Start it back up."

She pushed the button to play the movie. Clover snuggled up next to Dash and was asleep within minutes. The stress of the day had evidently taken a toll on her.

Dash pointed to the sleeping child and whispered, "I'll carry her into her room."

Grace nodded, smiling as she watched his broad shoulders working to lift her little girl and carry her to bed. She hurried ahead of them to pull the covers back out of the way. Once Clover was settled, Grace tucked the blankets around her and leaned down to kiss her forehead.

When she stood back up, she couldn't quite believe the way Dash was looking at her. Even in the semi-darkness, she could see that his bright blue gaze was filled with admiration, warmth, and a spark of something else.

Shaking her head as she walked out of her daughter's room, she tried to decide if she was simply attributing her own growing feelings to Dash. She couldn't deny how nice it was having a strong, caring man to help with Clover and to simply be there through all of life's ups and downs. It would be amazing to have a permanent male fixture in their lives, but Grace knew that couldn't be Dash. Once they found Star, and Dash went back to living his own life, this happy little family façade with him would end.

When they settled back in the living room, Grace lifted the remote to turn off the television.

Dash gave her a surprised look before nodding. "We should finish it with Clover."

Grace couldn't help chuckling at the silly man. He had evidently been willing to finish watching the cartoon, even though it was just the two of them now. It also wasn't lost on her that he used the word 'we', as if he expected to be around when they finished watching the movie. She tried not to grasp onto that word with too much hope.

Knowing she needed to protect the few remaining walls around her heart, she steeled her resolve by reminding herself where he was this morning when Star disappeared.

"We both know your time here is limited, and I doubt if chef Emily Hart watches a lot of Disney movies," she snapped, trying, but failing to keep the hurt feelings from showing in her voice.

Dash's face looked truly perplexed. "Emily?" He stared at Grace with his brow furrowed as he tried to process her meaning. Evidently giving up, he finally asked, "What does she have to do with anything?"

Grace knew she didn't have any right to be jealous. She and Dash weren't in an exclusive relationship--or any romantic relationship at all. Knowing it and controlling her reaction were two different things, though.

"I know you were with her this morning when Star was abducted." Grace let the implication hang heavily in the air that if he had been with the puppy, like he was supposed to be, she wouldn't have been stolen.

"You know about that?" Dash looked stunned that someone had revealed his whereabouts to her.

Grace merely lifted her brows and nodded in response. She wasn't justified in her anger, but her knowledge of that fact didn't make her simmering irritation any less real.

"I was hoping to surprise you." Dash sounded disappointed.

"Surprise me?" Grace asked, perplexed as to why Dash thought his spending time with the beautiful and talented chef would be a surprise for her. If he honestly thought Grace would be thrilled to hear about his budding relationship with Emily, then he couldn't be more wrong.

Seeming to sense the conclusion Grace had drawn, Dash had the audacity to tip his head back and laugh. "Oh, no. It's nothing like that," he assured Grace before adding, "I asked her to teach me how to make lasagna."

Nodding, Grace couldn't deny his explanation made sense, but she still wondered if it was just a convenient excuse for him to spend more time with the classy chef.

The lingering concern must have shown in her eyes because Dash took one of her hands in his and looked down into her eyes. "Grace, I'm taking lessons from her because I want to make lasagna for you and Clover."

30

*G*race almost couldn't believe her ears. *The great Dash Diamond was taking lessons from the most renowned chef in town so he could cook for her and her daughter?* The mere idea of it would have seemed inconceivable mere weeks ago. None of this would have been possible if it weren't for Star.

Grace told him honestly, "Having you want to make lasagna for us is the best surprise I can imagine, and I can't wait to taste it."

Clearly in tune with her emotions, Dash prompted her to go on. "But?"

"But it feels wrong to be happy when Star is missing. I'm so worried about her."

"I know," he soothed her before putting a strong arm around her shoulders.

She tilted her head into his embrace. It felt so good––and foreign––to have a strong man to lean on when she needed support.

"I miss her, too," he admitted quietly.

Grace lifted her head so she could look into his eyes and

judge his sincerity. "Really?" she asked, not quite believing it.

Dash nodded before saying, "Yeah, somehow you, your adorable munchkin, and that ornery little puppy have wormed your way into here." He lifted her hand to place over his heart, pressing it into his chest with his own hand.

She delighted in his warm touch and noted that his heart was hammering in his chest almost as hard as her own was within hers.

"There might be a permanent spot in there for you," he said so quietly she almost wondered if she imagined it.

After a long silence, he changed gears by saying, "We'll find Star. I know it." His voice was infused with confidence.

"I hope so." Grace's voice didn't sound as secure. "I can't stand the thought of Clover dealing with the loss of her." She didn't bother to hide the tears that meandered down her cheeks as she leaned on Dash.

Dash pulled back and stared solemnly into her watery eyes. "I'll do anything in my power to make sure that doesn't happen. We will bring her home. I promise."

Even though Grace knew it wasn't logical, she believed him. In that moment, it seemed the only viable outcome was for Star to be safely returned to them. Any other alternative simply couldn't exist.

Her eyes were glistening as she looked at him, nodding and fully believing they would somehow find the little dog.

Dash leaned in close to her. Their lips were a mere whisper apart. They took a few breaths suspended there, savoring the moment just before their first kiss. Grace's eyelids drooped like they were weighted as they slowly drifted closed. She inhaled the scent of him, desperate to shrink the gap between their lips, yet captivated by his spell of lingering in the moment, drinking in its deliciousness.

She relished the heat of Dash's lips hovering over hers,

until a scratching noise came from outside her door. The spell broken, they both snapped back to look at each other.

"You don't suppose?" Grace asked the partial question, knowing they were both hoping the same thing.

"No way," Dash answered. Proving that he was, indeed, on the same wavelength as Grace, he stood and bolted to the window to peek out the curtain, evidently not wanting to give a wild animal access to the house.

"Star!" he yelled with relief and joy obvious in his tone.

Grace almost couldn't believe her ears. "What?" she asked, but she was already running for the door.

Dash beat her to it and flung the door open. Sure enough, Star was sitting there waiting for them to let her in. She was wet and dirty, but that didn't stop Dash from scooping her up and happily presenting her to Grace.

"You're home, sweet baby," Grace cooed at the puppy. Star happily burrowed her head into Grace's caress.

The three of them shared a long moment. Dash was holding Star, but he was using one his arms to encompass Grace in their embrace.

"Let's dry her off and take her in to Clover!" It was Dash who made the suggestion out loud, but it mimicked Grace's thoughts perfectly. She normally wouldn't wake the child once she was asleep for the night, but she knew Clover would sleep more soundly knowing their puppy was safe.

Nodding enthusiastically, they set about getting the filthy puppy cleaned up. "You've had a rough day, huh?" Dash ruffled Star's nape with a big fluffy towel.

Grace couldn't help but feel touched by how much Dash seemed to truly care about Star. He had done a complete about-face in his feelings towards her in a brief amount of time. Having the puppy be in danger must have made him realize how precious she was.

Once the puppy was reasonably clean and dry, Dash

carried her into Clover's room. Grace turned on her daughter's closet light to give them enough illumination to see, but not so much as to startle the sleeping child. Giving Clover's shoulder a gentle shake, she said, "Look who's home."

Clover had been sound asleep, so it took a moment for her heavy-lidded eyes to fully open and for her to get her bearings. When her mind clicked into gear, her face lit up like a Christmas tree.

"Star!" she squealed, holding her arms up for the puppy. Star wiggled and flapped her tail as Clover nuzzled her. "I missed you so much. I'm so happy you're home," the little girl told her dog.

Grace felt more tears——this time joy-filled——streaming in trails down her cheeks. "Sleep tight." She leaned down to kiss both of her girls' foreheads before turning to leave.

She flipped the closet light off and heard Dash say softly, "Good night, sweet girls."

Closing the door behind them, Grace realized she couldn't imagine being much happier. Amending her thought slightly, she decided actually getting that filled-with-promise kiss from Dash might send her spiraling right past cloud nine and up over the moon.

31

"I'm way too pumped up to sleep," Dash told her when they returned to the living room.

It was almost like he could read her mind because that had been exactly what she had been about to say.

As Grace was thinking how in tune they were with each other, Dash's next sentence proved that the desire to stay up late was where the congruence of their thoughts ended. "I'm so happy to have Star home, but now we need to focus on finding who took her."

Grace's thoughts had been on finishing their almost-kiss, but she had to admit Dash made a valid point.

Not sensing her inner struggle, he went on, "We sure don't want it to happen again."

She hadn't even thought of that possibility. Now that he had brought it up, bringing Star's captor to justice and making sure he never struck again drowned out any thoughts of kissing. That would have to wait. Right now, they needed to focus--before the kidnapper's trail went cold.

"Okay." She fired up the logical side of her brain. "It could have been a random audience member."

"I suppose," Dash admitted. "But the audience loves Star, and a million dollars is an obscene amount of money. It almost feels like it was an inside job of someone who knows the inner workings of the studio. Maybe someone who was jealous of Star?"

Grace didn't point out that he was the one who had been the most jealous of Star, since she no longer had any doubts about Dash's sincerity or his feelings for the pup.

Snapping her fingers, she suggested, "What about Evelyn?"

"Evelyn?" Dash seemed taken aback by the thought.

Defending the accusation, Grace said, "She's overworked and probably underpaid. She's grouchy and snippy, which suggests she's unhappy at her job." She could tell by his face that Dash wasn't convinced, so she added, "Besides, it's always the quiet ones you have to watch out for."

Leaning in, she added, "Even Clover had a bad feeling about her." Changing to a whispering tone, even though they were the only ones in the room, she said, "She calls her Evil-lyn."

Dash burst out with surprised laughter at the child's unflattering nickname for the production assistant. Once his laughter subsided, he said, "Evil-lyn has a bit of a crush on me. If she was going to abduct someone to lock up at her house, I don't think it would be the dog."

Grace guessed it was more than a 'bit' of a crush, but she appreciated Dash trying to downplay the other woman's feelings for him. His brushing off of Evelyn's crush on him didn't curb the flash of jealousy in Grace, though. She wasn't normally an envious person, so she didn't like this new, unfamiliar side of herself, but she didn't seem to have any control over it.

Wanting to move the subject away from the other woman, she asked, "What about Miles? He seems smarmy enough to try to profit from a puppy."

"He is rather materialistic," Dash weighed in, nodding and seeming to ponder the possibility. "My gut instinct has always been that he has a heart of gold buried deep under his slick exterior, though." Shrugging his shoulders, he added, "I could be wrong, but I don't think it was him."

Grace smiled up at Dash. He wanted to see the best in everyone. "You don't want to believe that anyone you know could have done this," she voiced her theory.

"Actually…" He held up his pointer finger to indicate he had an idea forthcoming. "I'm wondering if it might have been someone on the executive team at the studio."

Frowning at him as if he had lost his mind, Grace replied, "But they love Star and the ratings she brings in. Why would they abduct her?"

"What is the only thing everyone in Redwood Cove has been talking about all day?" he asked her practically.

"Star's puppy-napping." She said the words aloud as realization dawned on her. "Her abduction was publicity gold for the show."

Dash nodded, confirming that her mind was in the same place as his. Adding to his theory, he said, "If someone really took her for the ransom money, then how did she escape and get home so quickly? Doesn't it seem a little too convenient that she appeared at your door less than twelve hours after her abduction?"

His ideas made perfect sense, but Grace hated to think that the business people she had trusted her puppy with would do such a thing. "We definitely can't rule out the studio execs," she finally weighed in. "It sounds like they had a significant motive."

"We're not going to figure it all out tonight," Dash said,

before adding, "How about if you come to the studio tomorrow? You can watch for anyone acting suspicious, and we can dig around for clues after the show airs."

She hated to call-in to the bakery because she prided herself on being one of the grocery's most reliable employees, but she didn't want the trail to go cold on Star's abductor. Nodding her head, she agreed. "That's a good idea."

"Okay, then it's settled. Now, I need my beauty rest, and you're sitting on my bed." Dash gave her a not-at-all-subtle hint.

"Oh, right." She was rattled by his sudden shift. "Good night," she said before quickly scurrying to the solace of her bedroom. Once she had her bedroom door closed behind her, she leaned back on it.

Apparently, that delightful hint of an almost-kiss wasn't on his mind at all, even though it was suddenly all she could think about. Sigh.

*A*t the studio the next morning, Grace scrutinized everyone. She felt confident that someone would have a 'tell,' and she intended to see it.

Someone had arranged for her to have a chair in the same spot at the side of the stage where she and Clover had sat during Star's debut show. Today, though, instead of a hard, metal folding chair, she had a cushioned seat with arms. Feeling like a pampered queen as she took her seat of honor, she wondered if Dash had requested the luxurious chair for her. Just the idea of him doing something so thoughtful made her heart thump hard enough that she could hear it in her eardrums.

She didn't notice anything out of the ordinary with the pre-show activity. Evelyn had her ever-present clip-board, and she was scurrying around like a hamster on a wheel. Miles was barking orders into his phone, and Dash was schmoozing the in-studio crowd. His natural charm and charisma had them laughing and clapping with glee––especially when he gave them the news that Star had been safely returned. Grace could have sworn the group gave a collective sigh of relief before their cheers erupted.

Grace could tell that the show was getting ready to start by the increased flurry of activity. Everyone was frantically running around, with the exception of Dash, who seemed to be the only calm, cool, and collected one on the set.

Her heart sank as she realized that Nora had normally brought Star out by now to get her settled in her place for the beginning of the show. There was no sign of the trainer or the puppy. She took a deep breath, trying to convince herself that Star's grooming routine had probably taken longer than normal, due to how filthy she was from yesterday's misadventures.

Star couldn't have been abducted again, could she? Surely, everyone in the studio was keeping a close eye on her. Grace suddenly felt like a bad pet parent for allowing Star to return to the scene of the crime. No amount of money or fame was worth risking their sweet little puppy.

She breathed a deep sigh of relief when Nora emerged from the back. Star was with her, but instead of loping along on her leash, she was being carried in a crate.

An uneasy feeling swept over Grace. She was supposed to be looking for anything out of the ordinary, and this was definitely odd. *Why would Nora have put Star into a crate?*

The answer to that question became clear when the woman set the crate down and tried to get Star out. When she reached in to get the puppy, Star growled at her. Grace had never heard the little puppy make such a noise before, but there was no denying what it was.

Grace sat up straight in her chair, watching Star and her trainer with wide, skeptical eyes. Something was definitely amiss.

Nora managed to get Star out of the carrier, but the puppy whirled around on her and bit at the leg of her dress pants. Star was often playful and ornery, but this was different. She sounded angry.

Grace's eyes shot to Dash. He was looking at her with the same stunned, knowing gaze that she aimed in his direction.

When Nora plopped Star on the couch and turned to leave, the puppy immediately calmed. Dash walked over, sat down, and quietly spoke to the dog as he gently scratched her head. She nuzzled up into his touch, obviously back to being her usual, loving self.

It was obvious then that Star was trying to tell them something. As much as Grace couldn't believe it, it was starting to look like Star's friendly, seemingly-loving trainer had something to do with the pup's abduction.

Dash was holding Star, not seeming to care that she was getting fur all over his suit, when the show started. He softly rubbed the white patch on her chest while he spoke. His entire monologue that comprised the first segment of the show was dedicated to assuring the audience that Star had been safely returned and sincerely thanking them for helping to look for the missing puppy.

He seemed like he was talking to each person individually as he spoke into the camera and made a plea for help in finding the person behind Star's puppy-napping. Grace wanted to scream at him that it was obviously Nora, but she wasn't sure about interrupting the show. *What if her hunch was wrong and she wrongfully accused an innocent woman on live television?*

She warred with herself as she listened to Dash convince his entire army of Redwood Cove viewers that the culprit needed to be brought to justice. She didn't want to risk having Nora escape, but she wasn't confident enough in her gut instinct to publicly blame her. She needed to talk to Dash to make sure his guess was in alignment with hers, but it seemed like an eternity before the first commercial break.

Grace had been worried she would have to fight her way to him, but Dash made a beeline for her as soon as the show went on break. "Come with me." It was more of an order than a request as he took her hand and led her to the side of the studio where he entered and exited.

Unable to keep her suspicions in check any longer, Grace stage whispered to him, "I think it was Nora." Simply uttering the words out loud felt scandalous, since the mild-mannered puppy trainer was the last person in the world anyone would suspect, but Star's reaction to the woman had majorly shifted.

Proving that he read the puppy's message loud and clear, Dash said, "I agree."

Grace sagged with relief that she wasn't just being a paranoid overly-suspicious mama bear about the situation. "What are we going to do about it? We can't let her get away with this," she hissed.

Dash nodded in agreement. "My friend, Bruce, is a detective on the police force. I'll have him check it out," he promised, already pulling up the man's number on his cell phone. "In the meantime, we can't let her know we are on to her, or she might try to make a run for it. We need to keep things business-as-usual." He gave Grace a pointed stare as if he could tell she desperately wanted to punch the dog trainer in the jaw.

Grace didn't have a violent bone in her body, but when someone she cared about was threatened, she didn't hold back. She nodded to acknowledge that Dash was right. They would have to keep a low profile with their theory about Nora until they had proof.

The trainer was standing near the sofa where Star was chewing on a giant bone. Normally, Nora whisked the puppy away during commercial breaks. Glaring in their direction, Grace decided something was definitely off between them.

Dash completed the call to his buddy, nodded to assure Grace that the police were on the case, and strolled back over to his spot in front of the camera just in time to resume the show. It was almost as if he had an innate sense of how long the breaks lasted.

Now that she had confirmation that Dash suspected the same thing she did, it was all Grace could do not to make her way around the set to confront Nora. She knew she should let the police handle it, but she feared going through the proper channels would take too long. She didn't want to give the woman time to escape.

Jitters had Grace tapping her feet as she tried to decide what to do. She couldn't even focus on the show because all she could think about was catching Nora. It seemed like an eternity before the next commercial break.

As soon as Dash signed off, promising the viewers that he and Star would be right back, Grace bolted out of her chair. Dash met her half way and led her back to their quiet spot at the side of the stage.

"She's going to get away." Grace knew they didn't have long to chat, so she led with the fear at the top of her mind.

"No, she isn't," he promised as he pulled out his cell phone. Glancing at the screen, he said, "Bruce already tracked down her home address. He's on his way there now to look around."

Grace was relieved to hear Bruce was taking their tip seriously and responding with urgency, but she couldn't imagine what he would find without a warrant to enter the property, She knew from television crime shows that those took a while to get.

When she voiced her concern to Dash, he smiled and said simply, "Bruce is very resourceful." With that reassurance, he strolled back across the stage and slid into his spot right as the show resumed.

As much as Grace wanted to believe in Dash's friend's investigative abilities, it was all she could do not to race to Nora's house in search of her own clues. As she tapped her fingers on her legs for the duration of the show, she came to the decision that as soon as the show ended, she would do some digging of her own.

33

As soon as Dash did his signature sign-off, with the addition of lifting Star's right paw to wave goodbye to the camera, Grace darted over to the sofa where her puppy was lounging.

Dash had gone out to the crowd to sign autographs and take selfies, but they normally didn't let the puppy do that, since the flurry of attention was overwhelming for her.

Grace scooped Star into her arms and turned to face Nora, who had just emerged from her hiding spot behind the couch. It wasn't lost on Grace that the woman was no longer needed to keep the puppy in order. Dash was able to wrangle her just fine on his own now. Besides, even when she misbehaved, her ornery puppy antics were adorable crowd-pleasers.

Turning a brittle smile in Nora's direction, Grace gritted her teeth, but tried to insert some friendliness into her voice. "I'm going to take Star with me today. She's had a rough couple of days." She added the explanation because she didn't want the woman to become suspicious about the change in Star's normal routine.

Star let out a low, muffled growl in Nora's direction, so Grace rubbed the pup's back in an attempt to soothe her. "Oh my." Grace tried not to sound too snarky. "I've never seen her react that way to anyone."

"It's normal." The trainer tried to brush aside the puppy's uncharacteristic behavior. When Grace was unable to keep the look of disbelief off her face, Nora changed gears. "You're just playing, aren't you, Star?"

When Nora reached over to ruffle the fur on the puppy's head, it took all of Grace's strength not to rip Star away from her. She managed to refrain only because she didn't want to let the trainer know they were on to her scheme. When Star burrowed up into Grace's neck in an attempt to get away from Nora's touch, the last tiny shred of doubt in Grace's mind fell away.

She knew in her heart Nora had something to do with Star's capture. Now, she just had to figure out how to prove it.

"I guess this means you get the rest of the morning off." She gave Nora her best fake smile. She knew the trainer sometimes worked with Star on basic obedience commands for a little while after the show, but she wasn't about to hand the puppy over to the woman, who she now believed to be a criminal.

"I guess." The woman returned her smile, but it didn't reach her eyes. She assessed Grace with her gaze. Grace hoped her true feelings couldn't be read on her face.

"There you are." Dash walked up and put his arm around Grace. "I've been looking all over for you." He gave Grace a pointed look, silently warning her not to confront Nora.

Grace gave him her best, innocent 'Who me?' look, but he didn't appear to be buying it.

"I have a couple of things to take care of in my office upstairs, then we can take Star on that walk along the boardwalk trail through the dunes, like we planned." He smiled and tried to steer Grace, who was still holding Star, away from Nora.

They had just turned away when Nora offered, "I'll keep an eye on Star while you take care of your business upstairs."

"No!" Grace reacted a little more strongly than she would have liked.

Smoothly covering for her, Dash gave Nora his best TV host smile and said, "Thank you, but that won't be necessary." Laying it on thick, he added, "It's a beautiful day out there; you should go outside and enjoy it."

Nora eyed them both warily. She seemed to sense something was off about their behavior.

Grace was beginning to wonder if the other woman was going to make a run for it when a man in an ill-fitting suit, followed by two uniformed police officers, barged into the studio. The trio quickly walked over to where Dash, Grace, and a stunned-looking Nora were standing.

The leader flashed a badge before loudly announcing, "Nora Flint, you are under arrest for the abduction of the star of the *Good Morning Gold Coast* show."

Dash cleared his throat and said loud enough for any nearby crew or straggling audience members to hear, "Now, Bruce, let's be clear here... Her name is Star. She isn't THE star of the show."

The implication that Dash was the true star hung heavily in the air. Grace rolled her eyes at this egomaniac, who was so different from the man that laughed and played with Clover at her house. "You keep telling yourself that," she blurted out.

She half-expected Dash to be angry with her for strongly implying that the puppy was the true star of the show, but his gaze at her held no annoyance.

"I knew that would get you going," the detective said,

jovially clapping Dash on the back.

Snapping her attention back to Nora, Grace realized the woman was about to make a break for it. "Get her!" she shouted and pointed, unwilling to let the criminal slip away without being punished.

Nora tried to bolt, but the cops were too fast for her. They had her cuffed and began reading her Miranda rights before she made it two steps away from their little gathering.

"Take her on out to the car, Kurt," Bruce said to one of the officers. He spoke to Nora as she went by, "Here's a free tip for you... The next time you decide to make a ransom note, don't put the cut up magazines in your trash can."

She glared in answer, which made the others chuckle at her rookie mistake.

Turning serious, Dash asked Nora, "Why did you take Star? We all thought you loved her."

The woman's expression held no shame when she spat, "You think I like crouching behind a couch while that little rat gets to be on camera, making ten times the paycheck I do?"

Grace almost answered that yes, it would be a pretty cushy gig, but she decided the bitter woman was beyond listening to reason.

Shaking his head in disgust, Dash said to his friend, "Make sure she's put away for a long time."

"And that she never works with animals again," Grace added.

Nodding, Bruce said, "We're on it."

Turning to grin at Grace, Dash said, "Told you Bruce was resourceful."

"You'd be surprised what you can learn about people by digging through their trash," Bruce informed them.

Dash wrinkled up his nose in distaste. "We'll take your word for it."

34

Once the others left, Grace was overtaken by nervousness. She wasn't sure why, but she felt compelled to say, "Anyone can easily see how much you've bonded with Star. I bet the studio bigwigs won't mind if you don't finish out your week at our house."

She could have kicked herself as soon as the suggestion was out of her mouth, but she knew it had been prompted by some innate need to protect her family from being hurt even worse when Dash inevitably left them for bigger and better things.

Dash's sparkling blue eyes gazed down into hers. "What if I want to finish the week with you?" he asked her, before adding, "Or perhaps even longer?"

Grace's heart leaped into her chest. She hadn't dared to hope that he would choose to spend time with them once it was no longer required of him.

"I suppose that can be arranged." She tried to sound coy, even though she wanted to leap for joy. Deciding to add a requirement, she continued, "As long as it's the real you, rather than the conceited Dash Diamond persona you adopt when you slip into vain celebrity mode."

"I've never felt more real than when I'm with you," he told her sincerely, not seeming a bit upset about her chastising his alter ego. "You make me feel like the real me is enough… like I don't need the celebrity façade."

Tilting her head back to smile at him, she said, "You are enough. The *real* you will always be enough for us."

He was gazing down at her with such fondness she wondered if he might tip his head down and give her that promised kiss. There were still a few people milling around, but Grace felt like she and Dash were the only two people in the entire world. Oh, and Star, of course, who was cradled in her arms like a sleepy baby.

"We should get going," he suggested, and the special moment passed, without a kiss.

Trying not to show her disappointment, she nodded. "Shall we walk, since it's so nice?"

He answered her question with his own. "You don't mind stopping for our adoring fans?"

Grace was touched that he had openly admitted Star was a big draw for people, too. Thinking it over, she decided it really didn't bother her to share the famous duo with the world––as long as she and Clover got them to themselves at home. "Not at all," she answered him, smiling to let him know she meant it.

Their walk was surprisingly peaceful. Other than a couple of autograph seekers and one lady who tried to sneak a snapshot, they were left alone.

It was a cool and foggy day. Dash used the dampness as an excuse to wrap his arm around Grace. She gladly burrowed into his warmth as they took the scenic route past gift shops, seafood restaurants, and bars that thrived in converted canneries along the waterfront.

The 'For Sale' sign in the window of the bridal boutique caught Grace's eye. A vision of herself and Dash having a lovely wedding by the sea popped into her head, but she had no business dreaming of that just yet, so she decided to put those thoughts out of her mind by asking Dash the question that had been bothering her. "How do you suppose Star got free from Nora and came home?" Deciding to toss in her best theory, she asked, "Did someone rescue her and leave her on our doorstep?"

She noticed the use of the word 'our' too late to suck it back in. She didn't want to push him to a place he wasn't ready to go, but if Dash noticed the slip, he didn't call her out on it.

"Maybe," he said noncommittally, before adding a theory of his own. "Or perhaps she made a break for it and found her way home, like pets do on all those sweet kids' movies."

"She's just a puppy." Grace shook her head, unable to believe Star might have returned home on her own.

"Yes, but she's super-smart and a bit of an escape artist," Dash defended his idea. She certainly had a way of getting through any barriers he put in the way to keep her from attacking his shoes during the show.

It was the first time Grace had heard Dash brag about Star. His obvious love for the pup made her heart feel like it was going to swell right out of her chest. "She is." Grace agreed with his assessment, before saying, "I sure wish she could tell us how she got home, but I guess we'll never know for sure. I'm just glad she's back."

"Me too," Dash nodded before changing the subject. "The wind is starting to kick up. How about if we order a car and run a few errands before we head home?"

His use of the word 'home' in reference to Grace's apartment made her want to jump with joy, but she managed to refrain. Instead, she nodded enthusiastically as she pondered spending the day with Dash.

Her logical brain told her to hold onto that last shred of protection around her heart, but Dash was making it extremely difficult.

35

*W*hen the car brought them home, the trio went together to Marlene's side to fetch Clover. It was the first time Dash had been to Marlene's place, and it quickly became obvious the woman was flustered and nervous to have the celebrity in her space.

Brushing at the flour on her cheek and shoving a wayward lock of hair behind her ear, she asked formally, "May I get you something to drink?"

Wanting to put her at ease, Grace said, "I'd like my usual, please," before plopping down on her stool at the counter, as she would on any other day.

The kids all ran out to fawn over Star. The puppy happily loped after them when they returned to the playroom.

"That little dog has quite a fabulous life." Dash shook his head, obviously thinking that Star had it made.

Not letting him get away with that, Grace reminded him, "Umm, so do you."

Dash didn't have to think about it long. "That's true," he agreed with her assessment before adding near her ear, "We're both so lucky to have found you."

A delightful chill raced down Grace's spine as his hot breath tickled the area right behind her earlobe. She closed her eyes to savor the feeling. When she reopened them, she realized Marlene had stopped stirring the chocolate chip blondies she was getting ready to bake.

The look Marlene was giving Grace spoke volumes. It was filled to the brim with sheer happiness. Grace could tell Marlene was starting to approve of Dash, and his place in their lives.

Wanting Marlene to be as comfortable with Dash as she was, Grace suggested, "How about if you and Dan and the kids come over for dinner some night this week?"

Dash jumped in and offered, "I'll make lasagna for everyone. I have a terrific recipe from gourmet chef Emily Hart that I want to try. She trained me to make it herself." He turned his sparkling gaze to Grace to let her know he was intentionally trying to rile her up.

When Grace simply narrowed her gaze in his direction, he changed gears. "The pan will be too much for just our little family, so this is a meal meant for extended family."

Hearing Dash refer to the people she cared about the most as 'family' made Grace feel like her heart wouldn't be able to handle any more happiness.

Any tiny bit of lingering doubt about Dash had been washed away from Marlene's expression when she responded with a genuine smile, "Lasagna sounds great."

They hadn't realized Clover had returned to the kitchen, until she chimed in with, "I love lasagna!" She said the word with a hard 'g,' which made them all chuckle.

Dash proved himself to be an insider in their little part of the world by saying, "It has cheese, please!"

They all laughed at that, then Dash, Grace, Clover, and Star said their goodbyes and went to their own side of the duplex.

When they walked in, Dash removed his shoes and plopped down on the sofa with a relieved, "Ahh... There's no place like home."

*O*nce Clover was tucked into bed with Star dozing peacefully by her side, Dash and Grace snuggled together on the couch. They shared a long, comfortable silence before Dash asked her, "What is your dream, Grace Wilson?"

She wasn't sure if he was referring to relationship goals, and she didn't want to scare him off, so she went the safe route with her answer. "Someday, I'd like to open my own bakery. I've taken a few business classes at night at Gold Coast Community College, but at the rate I'm going, I'll probably never graduate."

"You're a real go-getter." Dash ignored her self-effacing comment as he leaned back to look at her. Focusing on the positive, he encouraged her to go on. "Tell me about your bakery."

She hadn't shared details about her bakery idea with anyone––not even Marlene, but once she started talking to Dash about it, the words kept flowing. "Well, it will feature all of the usual breakfast pastries––donuts, cinnamon rolls, croissants, fruit tarts…"

Dash interrupted her list by saying, "You're making my stomach growl."

Jumping to her big idea, she said, "Plus, we will have giant donuts."

She paused to gauge his reaction to her announcement. His brow was furrowed, which didn't exactly boost her confidence. "What do you mean giant donuts?" he asked her.

"I mean really big ones... Huge." She held up her hands about a foot apart to give him a visual. "People can take them to the office or to morning gatherings. Rather than everyone grabbing their own donut and going their separate ways, they can cut or break off a piece of one big donut that they all share."

She couldn't tell by his expression what he thought of her idea, so she justified it further. "It will be like a coffee cake, except it's a donut. Everyone loves donuts." By the end of her statement, her voice lost steam and trailed off. Her confidence in her idea wavered when she realized the only person she had ever shared it with looked incredibly uncertain about its viability.

"Huge donuts." Dash rolled the words around his mouth. He had a faraway expression as he pondered her idea. Finally, turning to give her his assessment, he said, "I love it! I would invest in that."

"Oh, I wasn't insinuating that you put any money towards it," Grace said quickly, horrified he had come to that conclusion.

"I know," he reassured her. "Besides, you don't need my money. You can use Star's earnings."

Grace shook her head. "I'm setting her money aside for Clover's college."

"All of it?" Dash seemed stunned by her revelation.

Nodding, Grace said, "It doesn't seem right to live off of my puppy's salary."

"You wouldn't be," Dash argued. "Her earnings would give you the initial start-up funds, but then your bakery would take off and earn a profit. I'm sure of it." He sounded super-confident. "Your bakery would be a legacy for Clover. Besides, you could pay the fund back once the bakery was on its feet, if you really wanted to."

Grace had never considered that her idea might truly become a reality. Owning a bakery had always seemed like a wild and crazy pipe dream--until now.

"I haven't even told you the best part," she teased him. Her eyes were alight with anticipation.

"Spill," Dash ordered, obviously anxious to hear the rest.

Excited to share the other half of her vision, Grace said, "One side of the bakery will be dedicated to gourmet, organic dog treats. People will be able to bring their four-legged friends in to pick out a bone or cookie, while they get their own sweet treat."

Grace thought she might burst while she waited for Dash to weigh in on her idea. When he finally enthused, "Brilliant!" the breath she hadn't realized she was holding rushed out of her with a whooshing sound.

Loving his reaction to her ideas so far, Grace went on. "I also want to donate any of the extra baked goods on the 'Sweets' side to a local nursing home. It drives me crazy to see all of the waste from the grocery's bakery that could be sent to people who need it and would appreciate it."

"You're so thoughtful." Grace's cheeks heated under Dash's gaze at her as he uttered the compliment. His obvious approval made her heart flutter with happiness.

Star had evidently decided to come back out to the living room to see what all the excited chatter was about because she chose that moment to let out a sharp bark.

Grace jumped at the noise, but quickly realized Star was staring at something in the corner of the living room. She didn't want the puppy to yap again and wake up Clover, so she quickly got up to investigate.

"Oh, it's a spider... a big spider!" Grace squealed as she pinwheeled her arms backwards, trying to get away from the eight-legged creature. Crossing to the far side of the room, Grace pointed towards the corner in question and turned to Dash. "Will you get it, please? I don't want to have to wake up Clover."

Dash gave her a stunned look. "You would wake that poor little girl to get up and take care of a spider for you?"

"I can't have it creeping around the house all night, sinking its fangs into us while we sleep." She knew her fear of spiders was irrational, but that didn't make it any less real.

"Well, you could get it, rather than disturbing Clover," he suggested rationally.

"I can't." She shook her head vehemently as she continued to point.

Seeing that she was truly scared, Dash let her off the hook. "I'll take care of it," he promised gallantly, before bending to pick up one of his shoes.

"No, don't smash it!" Grace practically yelled, before covering her eyes with her free hand. "Slide it onto a paper plate and take it outside."

As he walked past her with the offending spider on the plate, she leaned away as if it might jump on her. "Put it on the other side of the fence, please," she requested.

This made him chuckle. "Oh, so if we kick it off the property, it will know it's not welcome to come back."

"Maybe," Grace justified her thinking, even though she knew it was completely illogical. She stood at the window to watch and make sure Dash released the spider on the neighbor's property. Although he had seemed to think her request was crazy, he complied with it.

When he came back inside, he said, "One spider safely evacuated."

Grace bent down to praise Star. This was the second time the pup had alerted her to a dangerous spider in their midst. She seemed to have a real knack for it. "You are such a good guard dog! You let us know about that big, nasty spider, didn't you?" She nuzzled the puppy's soft fur with her cheek.

Dash looked flabbergasted. "What about me?" He pretended to be outraged. "I'm the one who got rid of the blasted thing."

Standing, Grace patted him on the back. "You did good, too." The patronizing tone was clear in her voice.

Sitting down on the couch, Dash pouted and pointed to his jawline. "Don't I get a snuggle?"

Joining him on the sofa, Grace rubbed her cheek lightly on his five o'clock shadow. "Ow! You're bristly!"

He tipped his head back and laughed at her overreaction. "There's one place on my face that I know doesn't have any stubble." He waggled his brows suggestively, letting her know he was angling for a kiss.

"Is that so?" she asked.

Even though a kiss was precisely what she wanted too, she had something that had been on her mind, and this seemed like the perfect time to bring it up. When he nodded enthusiastically, she said, "I make it a rule not to kiss a man until I know his name... his *real* name."

"That's probably a good rule," he agreed, before swiping his long fingers over his face.

They sat in silence for a long moment as Dash debated whether or not to tell her. Grace was practically bouncing with anticipation.

Evidently making his decision, Dash turned to face her and said, "You have to promise not to laugh."

"I won't laugh," she said seriously, even as she wondered how bad it was.

"No one in California knows my real name. Only people from my hometown have any clue what it is, and they have proven themselves to be loyal," he hedged. He seemed to be looking for an excuse not to tell her.

"I won't tell," she promised him, and she meant it. If he didn't want anyone to know his real name, it wasn't her place to share it.

Taking a deep breath for courage, he finally revealed, "My name is Orville Otto Otis."

Grace bugged her eyes out at him. "Oh, that's a lot of O's," she finally weighed in on his odd moniker.

"My mom was a big fan of alliteration. Just ask my sisters, Opal and Olive."

Smiling, she said, "I guess you are too… Dash Diamond."

"You're smiling," he accused. "You promised no laughing."

She could tell he was truly self-conscious about his name. Looking directly into his eyes, she said, "I'm not laughing, Orville."

The shift in his gaze was immediate. He went from looking anxious and self-conscious, to affectionate and adoring. "You know, everyone always expects me to be a certain way for the camera, but you let me be me."

It was the greatest compliment Grace could have imagined. She truly didn't care about the star-power or celebrity of Dash Diamond. She had fallen for the real man underneath that act.

"I feel truly at home when I'm here." He spread his arms to encompass the room. "With you," he added, bringing his hand down to caress her chin with his finger.

She gazed up at him, feeling pure joy at his revelations. "I can't imagine our home without you in it," she told him honestly.

"You don't have to," he promised her, tilting his face in close to hers.

Her voice sounded husky when she suggested, "I'd like to learn more about the part of your face that isn't scruffy."

It was all the invitation he needed. He leaned in to brush his lips lightly across hers. They stayed frozen for a long moment, savoring the electrifying magic of their first kiss.

His lips were soft, warm, and delightful. The kiss tingled all the way down to the tips of her toes.

He trailed his fingers along her cheek, and then they threaded into her hair. She decided in that precise moment that she would never get enough of the delicious sensations brought on by kissing this man.

When they finally broke apart, they hovered together for a long moment, gazing into each other's eyes.

"Wow." It was a simple, yet accurate assessment.

"Yeah," Grace breathed out, feeling almost as if she were captivated by a potent love spell.

One of the only things that could have pulled her out of her daze was the chewing noise coming from their feet. Concerned that Star was going to destroy more of her furniture, she pulled back to check on the puppy.

When Orville looked down and saw what she was chewing on, he let out a frustrated sound. "Aargh!" Holding up his mangled, expensive-looking Italian leather loafer, he asked, "When is she going to grow out of this chewing stage?"

"We'll find out together," Grace promised.

His destroyed shoe forgotten, Orville let it drop to the floor and nodded his agreement with Grace's bold suggestion.

They sealed the deal with a kiss. With that symbolic promise of idyllic days to come, their little family began creating their own present-day golden age of happiness.

EPILOGUE

*A*s much as Orville couldn't deny that he hadn't appreciated it when the naughty little puppy originally became his unlikely co-host, he also couldn't quite believe how much he had grown to care about Star in the time since. The adorable fluffy pup had won him over--especially as she grew in size and began to mature--but she wasn't the one who had completely stolen his heart.

That privilege belonged to the freckle-faced, gap-toothed little girl, who had the word 'love' right in the middle of her name. Clover Cherise Wilson only came up to his waist, but what she lacked in height, she made up for in gumption. That child could talk him into just about anything. Her exuberance when she got her way was contagious. Grace tried to tell him the little girl had him wrapped around her tiny pinkie finger. He firmly denied that, even though he secretly knew it was absolutely true.

While sweet Clover had his heart, her beautiful mother, Grace, held his soul. His heart skipped a beat every time Grace glanced in his direction. He wasn't sure how he had lived so much of his life without her, and he intended to never experience the absence of her in his life again. She completed him in a way he had never imagined to be possible.

Their courtship had been fast, thanks to his forced bonding time with Star, but he felt certain that it was more than a mere quick flash of passion. His love for Grace grew more intense with every passing day. It was the deep, enduring kind of love that he knew would last for a lifetime.

Somehow, lonely and desperate Dash Diamond had found a family to love that would love him right back. He could be himself around them, and they didn't judge. They loved the real him, and that knowledge gave him the confidence to drop his slick celebrity façade--even on the air.

The audience was really responding to the new and improved, humble and happy Dash Diamond. He wasn't ready to share his real name with the public just yet. He remained Dash at work, but he was now free to be Orville at home. His viewers sensed the shift in his attitude. Even though he hadn't specifically said it, the audience could tell he was in love.

With the absence of Nora, the show's producers had offered to hire a new trainer for Star, but he hadn't been comfortable turning their dog over to anyone else--especially considering her last trainer had puppy-napped her.

Instead, he volunteered to train her himself. The dynamic duo stayed at the studio every day for an hour or two after the show, working on simple commands like *Sit*, *Stay*, and *Heel*. Star was learning fast and growing every day. The viewers loved watching her change before their eyes--both in appearance and behavior.

The two hosts were completely in sync with each other, and it was obvious, to anyone who watched even five minutes of the show, they had forged an incredibly deep and loving bond.

Miles made a point of bringing up the fact that he was the one who discovered Star, whenever the opportunity arose. Dash would roll his eyes at the braggart, but he couldn't truly be annoyed with him, because Miles' insistence that Star join the show was the reason Dash now had his beloved family. If he lived a thousand years, he could never thank the producer enough for fighting to get Star on the show.

He watched the studio audience get warmed up for today's show. Butterflies fluttered in his stomach. It had been a long time since he had been nervous for a show, but today was special––in more ways than one.

When he jogged out to greet the crowd, Star trotted amiably by his side. She was on a leash, even though she didn't need to be. She knew her part of the routine. Her tail wagged as she sat down beside Dash and flashed her pearly-white teeth in what appeared to be a wide, happy smile at her adoring fans. There was no denying the photogenic dog had the kind of natural charisma and charm that couldn't be taught. She worked the audience like a true professional.

Without consciously thinking about it, Dash rested his hand on the crown of Star's head as he spoke directly to the crowd, thanking them for coming and telling them they were here for a very special show.

Looking down at Star with fresh eyes, Dash wondered when she had grown tall enough for him to reach her head without stooping. At some point, her snout had elongated––morphing her snub-nosed, adorable puppy face into that of a gorgeous dog.

He spent so much time with her, both at work and when he was at Grace and Clover's house, it was difficult to see the constant changes in her appearance, until he took a step back and remembered how she looked that first day he met her in the park.

Smiling, he remembered that was the day Clover had

kicked him in the shin. He hadn't stood a chance at resisting that little whippersnapper.

Ever the professional, Star nudged his hand to remind him it was time for them to take their places to start the show. She led the way to the sofa and they sat down together just in time for their cue.

This morning's monologue was a little different. He knew Grace would be too busy at the grand opening of her bakery to watch the show, so he let the audience in on a little secret... "I'm in love." He spoke directly into the camera as if he were making a revelation to his best friend.

The in-house crowd leaned in as he shared some juicy details about his private life. "Her name is Grace, and she is the most beautiful, kind, and caring person I have ever met."

Giving the camera one of his signature smiles, Dash added, "Ladies, I am officially off the market... for good."

He chuckled when the audience responded with good-natured groans of disappointment.

Turning serious, he added, "My wish for each and every one of you is that you get to experience this kind of joyful, life-affirming love. I never imagined it would be possible for me, so don't ever give up on it for yourself."

With that sage advice, he changed gears. "Now, most of you know I don't give out recommendations on this show... ever. If there's one thing I've learned in all my years hosting this program, though, is that rules are sometimes made to be broken. If my executive producer hadn't been willing to put his reputation on the line to make a mischievous little puppy my co-host, we wouldn't have gotten to meet Star." He rubbed his hand down the dog's shiny coat along her spine and turned from the camera to give Miles a quick nod of acknowledgment.

Turning back to the camera, he continued, "All of that to say... If you haven't tried a giant donut from Sweets and

Treats Bakery on Bay Street, you are missing out. They are delicious crowd pleasers."

As an afterthought, he added, "Oh, and you can pick up a Star-approved treat for your favorite pooch while you're there. Star personally taste tested each of the selections from the Treats side of the bakery and gave them two enthusiastic paws up."

Although he had never made a personal recommendation like this on the show, he had a feeling Grace's bakery was about to be inundated with more Gold Coast patrons than she would know what to do with. His on-air shout-out, along with a quick post on Reel Life, would get her business off to a booming start, and her phenomenal pastries, desserts, and treats would have people clamoring for more.

The rest of the show proceeded without a single hitch, and before he knew it, he and Star set off on the even more exciting portion of their day. They had a few stops to make before Grace closed the bakery after its debut day.

Once they finished their errands, he stopped by Marlene's to pick up Clover. Grace had texted she would be at work a little later than anticipated because she was organizing all of the orders that came in after they sold out on both the sweets and treats sides of her new bakery.

When he shared that news with Marlene, she said, "Her smashing success was in no small part due to your recommendation this morning." Her eyes were glimmering with approval in his direction.

"Maybe," he admitted. "But it's her delicious recipes that will keep them coming back for more," he predicted.

Marlene nodded her agreement with his assessment. Deciding to go all in, he told Grace's confidant the rest of his plans for the day. When the woman simply stared at him with wide eyes, a sliver of doubt began to creep in. He felt confident and ready, but he didn't want to rush Grace.

Finally, Marlene brought a hand up over her heart as tears of happiness welled in her eyes. She was too emotional to speak, so she merely nodded her approval.

He released the breath he'd been holding in a giant puff of air. After securing Marlene's agreement to play her role in his plan, he called Clover in from the playroom and asked if she had any interest in going to the park.

As expected, the little girl squealed with delight over that idea. He whistled happily to himself as he walked with Clover and Star towards their favorite playground and dog park by the bay. Everything was falling perfectly into place.

He sent a snapshot of Clover and Star playing ball at the fenced-in waterside dog park to let Grace know where to meet them when she finished at work.

She texted back, *I'll be there in 45 minutes. Had a GREAT first day!*

He couldn't wipe the grin off his face as he watched two of his favorite girls running and playing together. They hadn't slowed down a bit when two warm hands reached around to cover his eyes, and a familiar voice said, "Guess who?"

Even if he hadn't recognized her voice, he would have known her touch from that of a thousand others because of the zinging electricity that raced down his spine. Simply being near Grace made his nerve endings come alive.

Deciding to tease her a little, he said, "Chef Emily?"

She used one hand to smack playfully at his back.

"Evelyn?" he tried again, grinning from ear to ear at his own orneriness.

Grace moved around so he could see her face. Even though it was obvious he had been joking, one of her eyebrows was lifted in a look that he took to mean he better stop.

"Oh, it's the only woman for me," he said, beaming at her.

Her annoyed face morphed into a coy smile. "That's more like it."

She stood by his side at the fence, so he took the opportunity to snake his arm around her waist. Grace told him all about the smashing success of her grand opening as they watched their girls play fetch in perfect harmony. Star's retrieving nature seemed to have blossomed in the past few weeks. She didn't always want to give the ball back, but she couldn't seem to resist anything Clover wanted.

When the breeze from the water began to kick up, Grace shivered, despite his warm embrace. "Ready to go?" he asked.

"Good luck getting those two to leave." She tilted her head towards Clover and Star.

"I'll take care of it," he said confidently, before heading inside the enclosure.

He picked up the red ball, gave it a toss for Star, and leaned down to whisper in Clover's ear. Grace's face appeared to be in awe when Clover nodded enthusiastically before calling Star. The dog happily loped after her girl, and within seconds the trio joined Grace––ready to leave.

"You really need to tell me how you do that," Grace murmured near his ear as they walked.

"I can't reveal all my secrets." He grinned down at her before adding, "But we may need to plan a day of go-carts and ziplining at Pacific Adventures Amusement and Fun Center sometime soon."

He enjoyed her chuckle at his unapologetic bribe. As they walked on, he set his plan into motion. "Oh," he said, as if it had just popped into his head. "I bought a house."

Right on cue, Grace's brows furrowed as she processed this news. He had suspected she would be concerned about his bold announcement. She was probably wondering how far this house was from her place and why she hadn't had any input in the decision. Their relationship had certainly progressed to that point, but he had been so confident in his choice, he had gone for it as a surprise.

"Would you like to see it?" he asked innocently, pretending not to notice Grace's concerned expression.

"Yes!" Clover jumped into the conversation.

Grace looked stunned. When she nodded her agreement, he began to wonder if he might have gone too far. Deciding there was only one way to find out, he suggested, "Let's head there now."

When they continued on their path for a while without veering off in another direction, Grace finally commented, "It feels like we're heading towards our place at Marlene and Dan's house."

"Hmm," he responded noncommittally.

When they reached the house right next door to Marlene's, Orville came to an abrupt stop on the sidewalk. Turning to face the house, he waved his arms with a flourish and said, "Ta-da!"

He carefully watched Grace's face as she looked at the white clapboard row house with blue shutters with fresh eyes. "You're the one who bought this place?" She sounded like she couldn't quite believe he was the mysterious investor who had been sprucing up the fixer-upper.

Nodding, he said, "It simply needed some cosmetic work. The structure has great bones." He could barely contain his enthusiasm when he pulled the key from his pocket and asked, "Want to take a look inside?"

"Sure," Grace responded, her voice tinged with uncertainty about what this meant.

Man, child, and dog practically skipped up the steps to the house's wraparound porch. Grace walked slowly behind them with her eyes wandering as she slowly took it all in.

Once inside, Clover ran from room to room exclaiming over the hidden built-ins. "This would be the perfect place for my dollies to have tea!" she shouted when she discovered the cubby under the wooden staircase. After running up the stairs, she yelled back down to them, "I found my room!"

Visibly cringing, Grace apologized for her daughter's presumptiveness.

"I'm glad she likes it," he laughed at the child's exuberance.

With perfect timing, Marlene opened the screen door and poked her head in. "Knock-knock," she said aloud, rather than doing so with her hand.

"Come on in," he said jovially at the same time as Grace accused her, "You knew about this?"

Accepting his offer, Marlene answered Grace's question, "Just since this afternoon."

That answer seemed to appease Grace, so Marlene suggested, "Check out the kitchen. I would kill for that huge Viking oven and cooktop, but I'm sure you'll put it to good use." She winked at Grace before kneeling down to address Star. "I think you've grown since a few hours ago, sweet girl," she said to the excited dog.

Orville couldn't wipe the smile off his face as he watched Grace scurry to check out the kitchen. He wiped his damp palms on his pants legs, realizing the time was finally here. Nodding at Marlene, he followed the woman of his dreams into the kitchen.

"I am going to sneak over here and use this oven." Grace beamed at him as she trailed her hand over the polished steel surface.

"That's fine," he said, before suggesting, "or you could just come downstairs and use it whenever you want."

She turned a questioning gaze at him. With impeccable timing, Marlene sent Star in their direction. The dog entered the kitchen with her tail flapping back and forth as if she knew she was a part of something very important.

Grace bent down to look at her. "What do you have?" she asked the dog, hoping she hadn't gotten into anything she shouldn't.

"Hand," Orville gave Star the command they had secretly been working on.

Without hesitation, Star shoved the bag she had been holding proudly in her mouth into Grace's hand. She then sat down and turned her big brown eyes to look up at Orville to see if he approved of her trick.

"Good girl." He patted the dog's head in praise, which made her tail flap so hard it smacked loudly against the kitchen tile.

"What's this?" Grace asked, obviously bewildered by the entire scene. When she pulled the drawstring on the velvet bag and slid out the burgundy ring box, one of her hands went up to cover her mouth.

Bending down on one knee before her and clasping her free hand within both of his, Orville said, "For the first time in a long time, I feel accepted and loved exactly as I truly am. I used to think everyone expected me to be an obnoxious celebrity, so that is what I became. You, Clover, and Star have given me the confidence to drop that fake persona and be my true self."

Looking directly up into her eyes as tears blazed trails down her face, he went on. "You taught me to love myself, and you have forever changed my life for the better. I will never be able to repay you for that, but, if you'll have me, I want to spend the rest of my days loving you more with each passing moment and thanking you for being my rock."

Using one of his hands to take the ring box and flip open the lid, he said earnestly, "Grace Elaine Wilson, will you make me the happiest man alive by agreeing to marry me?"

Grace appeared too choked up to speak, so she merely nodded her head in answer. He stood and pulled her into an excited hug before letting out a whoop of pure happiness.

Marlene and Clover let out similar celebratory squeals as they peeked through the kitchen's pass-through window. Star's toenails clacked a happy dance on the kitchen tile–– almost as if she understood what a monumental moment this was.

When Grace pulled back and held out her hand in expectation, he slid the ring on her finger, saying, "Did you know engagement rings and wedding bands are worn on the third finger of the left hand because the ancient Romans believed the vein of this finger ran directly to the heart? They called it the 'vein of love.' Even though modern-day biology suggests that all of our fingers have connections to the heart, the tradition stands."

"Really? I've never heard that." Grace wiggled her fingers to watch the brilliant diamond sparkle in the sunlight.

Marlene and Clover scurried to join them in the kitchen.

"Let me see that rock," Marlene demanded jovially. "Perfect!" She gave Grace a nod of approval that encompassed both the man and the ring.

After hugging them both, she said, "I'll let your family explore your new home in peace." Bending to Clover's level, she asked, "Want to come over later for a movie night with my crew?"

When Clover nodded enthusiastically, Marlene stood to her full height and winked at Grace over the child's head, silently acknowledging her offer of some quiet time for the newly-engaged couple in their new home.

"Thank you," Grace mouthed the words at her friend.

Once they were alone, Grace, Orville, and Clover embraced each other in a three-way hug. Not willing to be left out, Star pushed her head into the family hug.

"I was thinking we could see if Muse would be willing to play at our wedding reception," Orville suggested.

"Wow, that would be fantastic––even if only one or two of them could make it––but all I really care about is getting to marry you," Grace weighed in.

Orville glanced down at Star, "Well, if I can't talk them into it, we'll sic Star on them. There's no way they could resist those big, brown, sweet puppy-dog eyes."

Grace nodded her agreement with that assessment, just before her face lit up with an idea. "Maybe we could get married at the Redwood Cove Inn. Think how lovely the pictures would be with those panoramic ocean views. Our guests could relax in the rocking chairs on their wraparound porch and enjoy the breeze coming in off the water." She could imagine it perfectly in her mind. Orville's smile let her know he was envisioning it as well.

None of them seemed willing to break their first real family hug, so they stood still for a long, quiet moment.

Clover was the first to break the silence. "When you guys get married, does that mean you'll be my Daddy?"

"Yes, sweetheart, that's exactly what it means... as long as that's what you want?" Orville's heart hammered in his chest as he waited for the little girl's answer. It was almost as nerve-wracking as anticipating Grace's response to his proposal.

Clover nodded enthusiastically. "Can we start now? Daddy?" She looked anxiously up at him.

"That sounds like a great idea," he told her, beaming with pride. His face took on a mischievous expression before he added, "You and I will work up all kinds of schemes to get even with Mommy for the time she put ice cream on my nose."

As Clover giggled and nodded, silently agreeing to his

plan, Grace tipped her head back to laugh at the silly man and said, "I thought you forgot about that!"

"We'll never forget, will we, Clover?" He used two fingers to point at his eyes. Then he indicated Grace as if to say he had his eyes on her.

Suddenly, the little girl brightened with an idea, "Come on, Star!" she said to her dog. "I'll show you the rest of our house."

The duo ran off happily together to explore. Grace and Orville shared a happy smile at their exuberance.

Suddenly seeming nervous that she wouldn't appreciate him making an enormous decision like this without consulting her, he said, "I didn't think you'd want to move far away from Marlene and her family, so when this house became available, I scooped it up before anyone else had a chance to make an offer on it."

He rubbed his sweaty palms down the front of his pants. "If it's not what you want, we can sell it and pick out something else together."

Smiling with reassurance, Grace told him, "It's perfect."

"Really?" Relief swept over his face.

Nodding, Grace confirmed, "Yes, it's exactly what I would have picked."

"Would you like to see the rest of the house... our house?" Orville amended the question, hoping she was as excited to see their new home as he was to show it to her.

"I would," she answered as she circled the kitchen, seeming to take in every detail from the spotless granite countertops to the shiny high-end appliances. It was obvious he had already put quite a bit of money into sprucing up the place, but he had left everything neutral, so she could add her own feminine touches to give it character and splashes of color. "I do have one question, though, before I can agree to move in here." She turned expectant eyes on him.

Orville swallowed audibly. Whatever it was, he would do anything in his power to make it happen. Unsure of his voice, he merely nodded for her to go on.

"Does the bathroom have a towel warmer? Because I don't think I can live without one." Her eyes sparkled with mischief as she resumed her spot directly in front of him.

"Who is the spoiled one, now?" he teased before answering proudly, "I already had them installed in all three bathrooms."

"Three bathrooms?" Grace sounded surprised.

Orville nodded in answer before saying, "And four bedrooms, in case we decide to give Clover some siblings."

Grace smiled up at him. "I like the way you think, Orville Otto Otis."

"It sounds like our future is set," he decided, before suggesting, "Shall we seal it with a kiss?"

"Absolutely," she murmured, before pressing her lips to his with the promise of forever.

Although they had believed their future to be set, Orville couldn't have imagined how wonderful the following years would actually be. He was living the life of his dreams, and it somehow managed to get better with each passing day.

Star had matured into a stunning, well-behaved, and kind-hearted adult dog. She was a dream of a co-host, who always hit her cues and seemed to have an innate sense of what needed to happen on the live show––even when things inevitably went wrong. The sweet dog was a steady and reliable best friend to Clover, and had become an integral member of their family.

Orville rubbed a hand over the slight bump on the top of Star's head as she leaned against the arm the couch, silently begging for his attention. He used his free hand to peruse email on his phone.

"Oh, there's a newsletter update from Mrs. Graves, and one of your littermates is featured!" He spoke to Star as if she could understand what he was saying because she seemed like she could.

Star's milk-chocolate brown eyes blinked up at him as if to say, 'Are you going to read it to me?' So, he quickly skimmed the email to give her the highlights.

"One of your canine sisters got an award from the mayor for finding a person who was lost on the Pacific Coast Trail!" His voice was filled with enthusiasm, which made Star's tail flap as if she could understand every word.

Leaning down to speak close to her face and rub her soft ears as she gazed lovingly up at him, he said, "It looks like you're not the only gorgeous and talented sibling from your litter, Miss Star."

The dog's mouth was open and her brilliant white teeth were gleaming. She looked almost like she was smiling with pride over her sister's grand accomplishment.

Overwhelmed with love for the dog he had fought so hard against accepting, Orville asked, "You know what, Star?" He spoke to her as if expecting an answer. When she just gazed back at him, he continued. "I think you might be the best thing that ever happened to me."

"AHEM," Grace cleared her throat loudly from behind him. She had evidently walked into the living room just in time to hear his admission.

Standing, he walked over to Grace. "She is." He defended his statement, which made Grace quirk a perturbed-looking eyebrow in his direction.

Deciding he better clarify before she really got angry, Orville said, "Without Star, I never would have met you—— the love of my life. I also wouldn't have my adorable, spunky, growing-like-a-weed daughter, or my soon-to-be-born son." He patted Grace's protruding belly that was beginning to make her look like she was smuggling a watermelon under her shirt.

"Nice save." She smiled up at him.

"My life is complete, thanks to Star." He couldn't resist teasing her. When she smacked playfully at his chest, he hastily added, "And you."

"Oh, I'm just an afterthought," she nodded, trying to look annoyed, but failing miserably.

"You're in all of my thoughts," he said huskily before tipping down to kiss her until they both forgot everything else.

WANT MORE SWEET ROMANCE
FEATURING LOVABLE DOGS?

Be sure to read *Goofy Newfies*, the sweet romance inspired by
Rocky & Cheerio (The big, loving, and goofy Newfies who
claimed me as their human).

GIVE A REVIEW. BEST. GIFT. EVER

Now is the time to help other readers. Many people rely on reviews to make the decision about whether or not to buy a book. You can help them make that decision by leaving your thoughts on what you found enjoyable about this book.

If you liked this book, please consider leaving a positive review. Even if it's just a few words, your input makes a difference and will be received with much gratitude.

LET'S STAY IN TOUCH!

Get VIP access. Be the first to know about new releases, sales, freebies, and exclusive giveaways. We value your privacy and will not send spam.

Visit annomasta.com to join.

EMAIL Ann to be added to her reader group:
author@annomasta.com

Made in the USA
Monee, IL
08 June 2023

35470975R00125